WARM THANKS

The first time Skye saw Natasha, he had mistaken her for a boy. But now she was soaked from wading the river, and there was no mistaking the proud breasts thrusting against her damp shirt.

"I never did properly thank you for saving my life," she said. She leaned forward, her shirt falling away from her cream-colored skin.

"No thanks necessary," Fargo said gruffly, thinking of her father and the other trappers nearby who would kill the man who fooled around with her.

"But I want to thank you," she said. Her arms went around his neck, her lips came hard against his.

Trying to hold her at bay, he said, "Fine. Now you've thanked me."

"Not enough," she said, and as her clothes came off, Fargo found it was damn hard to worry about playing with fire when you were enjoying the heat. . . .

THE TRAILSMAN 68

TRAPPER
RAMPAGE

by

Jon Sharpe

A SIGNET BOOK

NEW AMERICAN LIBRARY

PUBLISHER'S NOTE

This book is a work of fiction. Names, characters, places, and incidents either are the product of the author's imagination or are used fictitiously, and any resemblance to actual persons, living or dead, events, or locales is entirely coincidental.

NAL BOOKS ARE AVAILABLE AT QUANTITY DISCOUNTS
WHEN USED TO PROMOTE PRODUCTS OR SERVICES.
FOR INFORMATION PLEASE WRITE TO PREMIUM MARKETING DIVISION,
NEW AMERICAN LIBRARY, 1633 BROADWAY,
NEW YORK, NEW YORK 10019.

The first chapter of this book previously appeared in
The Manitoba Marauders, the sixty-seventh book in this series.

SIGNET TRADEMARK REG. U.S. PAT. OFF. AND FOREIGN COUNTRIES
REGISTERED TRADEMARK—MARCA REGISTRADA
HECHO EN CHICAGO, U.S.A.

SIGNET, SIGNET CLASSIC, MENTOR, ONYX, PLUME, MERIDIAN
and NAL BOOKS are published by NAL PENGUIN INC.,
1633 Broadway, New York, New York 10019

First Printing, August, 1987

1 2 3 4 5 6 7 8 9

PRINTED IN THE UNITED STATES OF AMERICA

The Trailsman

Beginnings . . . they bend the tree and they
mark the man. Skye Fargo was born when he
was eighteen. Terror was his midwife, ven-
geance his first cry. Killing spawned Skye
Fargo, ruthless, cold-blooded murder. Out of
the acrid smoke of gunpowder still hanging
in the air, he rose, cried out a promise never
forgotten.

The Trailsman, they began to call him, all
across the West: searcher, scout, hunter, the
man who could see where others only looked,
his skills for hire but not his soul, the man
who lived each day to the fullest, yet trailed each
tomorrow. Skye Fargo, the Trailsman, the
seeker who could take the wildness of a land
and the wanting of a woman and make them
his own.

*Late spring, 1859—in Washington Territory,
that vast open-game wilderness of the far Northwest,
where trappers snared furbearing animals
and hunters stalked furbearing trappers . . .*

1

The bend was a bitch.

Stroking hard against the swift current, Skye Fargo rowed upriver through the rock-fanged turn of the cascading Okanogan, grimacing as water sloshed over the gunwale of his light but laden skin canoe. Afternoon sun slanted under his tall-crowned hat, giving his black-bearded face a bold, aggressive appearance; the broad brim shaded his lake-blue eyes while he gauged the torrent ahead.

At the crook of the curve was a wedge-shaped hillside, whose steep yet overgrown slopes thrust out from the eroded west bank like the prow of a ship. The river hooked sharply around the hilly point, cutting a hazardous channel of writhing flows, jagged outcrops, and submerged ledges. True, compared to rapids like the Columbia's and Mad River's Dance of Death, this Okanogan patch was no great horror. But all were treacherous, ready at a moment's lapse to sink or kill.

The Okanogan almost succeeded in claiming Fargo in those next furious moments, the thin-skinned canoe tossing and yawing, shipping water, and more than once Fargo was sure it was holed or staved in. But it continued its wild progress with no detectable leaks, rounding the bend and reaching the final fringe of cataracts. Relieved, he threaded the last stony tiers. Intent on them, squinting through ob- scuring spume with the white-water roar loud in his ears, he almost missed the opening play.

Fargo was swinging his blade high to clear the frothy head of a close-by rock, when in the same instant he glimpsed a smoky cloud belch from the hillside, heard the harsh crack of a long rifle, and felt the paddle almost ripped from his grasp. He jerked, startled . . .

But not surprised.

Along the Columbia and its tributaries gossip had been floating of some unseen force preying on free trappers—independent fur men under no bond to any post or factor. No facts—only barfly rumors, and dark wagers that before midsummer, death and the devil would cross paths with many of the trap- pers who weren't under contract. Fargo had heard this and much other bunkum on his way here, and normally he'd just forget it. His journey, though, was in response to a note from a free trapper, his old friend Modoc Doyle:

Years are creeping up on me and the fires of a younger scalawag might keep lonely camps warm.

Doyle couldn't write, Fargo knew. Whoever he'd hired must have specialized in lovesick letters to have penned such drivel, but the casual tone was strictly "Never Ask" Doyle's. No matter; the mes- sage was in the sending, for Doyle resorted to notes only in direst calamities. He was howling for help.

Fargo could not refuse. He'd ridden west quickly, and knowing he could make better time and get a sense of what trouble was brewing, he had taken to the river. His trusty Ovaro was stabled in the small town growing up outside Fort Walla Walla, en- trusted to a hosteler glad to see such a fine piece of horseflesh. Fargo felt uneasy without the pinto and always the wary wolf, he had liked the feel of things en route less and less, despite no evidence and all the signs of peace. Camping, he'd slept on his guns, in coverts that commanded his beached canoe, and voyaged with his Sharps and Colt revolver stashed near, easily reached.

Reach he did now, fast. Whipping in the paddle, whose blade showed a splintered edge and a dark burn of lead, Fargo grabbed for his revolver, which he'd kept primed and powder-dry in a tuck of oilcloth. The range was long. In a bucking canoe, though, the single-fire Sharps would be nasty to reload, and its recoil might well dump over the whole caboodle.

Thumbing the gun hammer, eyeing the breeze-blown powder cloud, Fargo was bringing his Colt to bear when flame and smoke erupted from the same low niche in yonder slope. He ignored the slug that whined past his ear, firing at the flash point three times—one shot just above it, two farther down, left and right, forming a tight triangle. It was a hard pattern to escape, even when shooting blind.

Through the reverberating gun thunder, Fargo thought he detected a faint cry of pain, a sort of stridently barked *wagh!* He had no chance to make sure or hear more, lurching as the canoe, caught by the current, careened back downriver. Snatching up the paddle again, he battled for the bank, straining as he twisted his blade in a turning effort. The canoe shuddered, swerved across current, then angled shoreward before it could be sucked any deeper into the rock-studded curve.

Fargo drove the craft high on the gravelly shingle, leapt out, and ducked into the bordering thickets. Keeping low, he dipped a little farther down the river bend until he was sure he was beyond the view of the ambusher's niche, then began up the slope of ponderosa, bitter root, and briar brush. Also up there was a rifleman, maybe wounded, maybe dead, maybe not alone. There'd been two reports, the first sounding like a Kentucky "Long Tom" musket, the second seeming to have the heavier, throaty blast of a percussion breechloader. Whatever, there had to be two rifles—nobody could cap and fire as rapidly as those shots had come. So two men, maybe, or one with a backup gun, but in any case holding a powerful drop on the river.

In a circuitous route, Fargo climbed cautiously to the niche through the shifting sunlight and shadows of foliage, the resinous scent of pine heavy about him. Soon ahead loomed a huddle of stone and bush, hedging an outward jutting spur of the hill. Crouching still, he caught no sound or motion from there, but his gut said that was the niche. That was enough for him to zero in on as he snaked through the undergrowth and slid between the cracked boulders.

Stealthily parting the brush, Fargo saw a V-shaped ledge overlooking the point. The small clearing was empty, save for a rifle lying in a splatter of blood. Across, a path continued on around the slope and led, he supposed, to the riverbank above the bend. If it did, and if the rifleman was wounded, as it appeared, then he or they might have fled that way, might be hitting the water right now.

Might not be, either. Warily Fargo rose out from the rocks. Retrieving the rifle, a newer Greene capping carbine, he saw a star branded in its stock, the mark of the Yankee Fur Company. Suspicions mounting, Fargo raced with it out of the clearing and along the path, which shortly dipped winding down the hillside.

The bank directly below was screened by tree-laced thickets. From the path's higher vantage, though, an eighth of a mile or so of river was visible, up to where it came pouring around another turn. No boats rode the straight stretch. Fargo cursed, running on, aware that in the time it'd taken him to reach the niche, a good fur company craft could have covered that small a distance.

The descending path then passed the thickets, and Fargo caught sight of a camp on the bank, with a sturdy *perique* tied to a pile of drift. That must be the outfit of the wounded ambusher, he figured. But as he approached, it looked more puzzling. A coffeepot sat on the cook fire beside a fry pan of fresh trout fillets, but the fire was cold, the wind toying with the dead ashes. A few other provisions were left about and a bedroll was spread nearby, unslept in. Of humans, there was none to be seen.

Going to water's edge, Fargo leaned out and grabbed the gunwale of the perique, craning to look in. Abruptly he chilled, staring at the body sprawled in the bottom. It was Joel Pegase. Fargo recognized the weather-cured, woodswise features of the free trapper, despite his throat being slit from ear to ear and coagulating blood all over everything. And protruding from his chest was the beaded haft of an Indian-trade skinning knife, ornately decorated after the manner of the Nez Percé. In the bow were the indubitable marks of a load of furs, missing now.

Gingerly he wrapped Pegase in the bedroll. Adding the rifle, he carted the grisly bundle back along the bank to his canoe, feeling rage and loss. Although not close friends, he'd found Pegase a likable cuss, and in the tradition of great mountain men, a heroic drinker and inspired dirty jokester. Now that ribald spirit was snuffed, killed for his winter catch while en route, Fargo was sure, to Modoc Doyle's camp. Somehow it seemed fitting to take him there, to let the trapper finish his final voyage.

After stowing the cumbersome bedroll, Fargo shoved into the current. His canoe wallowed over-stuffed, but digging deep, he cleared the bend and plowed on up by Pegase's fatal campsite. It was then that he spotted the motion beyond, other craft sweeping around the curve ahead.

Hastily backing water, he stalled for a second while trying to take their full measure. Five stout wood *bateaux*, he counted, hurtling to the thrust of eight strong paddles. The crews were indistinct, though he doubted they were Indian, glimpsing the sort of buckskin and mackinaw jackets worn by northern frontiersmen. Apparently they spied him, for suddenly the *bateaux* bristled with rifles like quills on a porcupine.

Spinning about to face downstream, Fargo saw one thing clearly: they had him by the short hairs. His blade bent and his muscles bulged beneath his close-fitting buckskin as he raced with the flow, back toward the cascading turn and, hopefully, to the swift channel below. A single miscue would bring disaster. He wasn't familiar with the Okanogan, but odds were the men storming behind him worked hereabouts, knew every mood and hazard, making passage seem easy while he struggled. For the same reason doubled, he should avoid the land. He'd be stuck on foot out nowhere with limited arms, against men of varying skill, perhaps, but lots of them, who were at home in this region.

There was one other thing to do: give up. That might be the smart move. It was possible they were chasing the wrong man. Hardly seemed as if they'd be launching a war fleet just to get him and—Fargo jerked, yanked by the whang cord of his hat, and smack dab through the crown was drilled the burning tunnel of a big-bore slug. Give up? What a laugh. They were out to get him, and get him good.

The canoe pitched and bucked when it struck the

bend. Hunching upright, bracing for balance, Fargo maneuvered the blade like a rudder while careening back into the rock-ribbed tumble. He tried not to flinch as rifles sounded faintly, and bullets spat little geysers or ricocheted off stone alongside, keeping focused on steering through the maze of the torrent.

Slewing, he made the point and cut from view. The gunfire tapered off as he swerved around the hazards of the lower curve, the rearing canoe quieting when finally the course straightened. With paddle thrashing madly, he tore onward, hoping to gain the next turn or at least some distance before his pursuers caught sight of him again.

The river ahead twisted in a lazy S. Fargo was verging on the upper angle when he glimpsed the *bateaux* breaking out of the bend behind, and for a moment lead slapped the water about him. Then again he was hidden, the swift channel flanked by overhanging oak, hemlock, and white fir. But again not for long, he knew. With quick darting eyes, he searched for an escape.

Spotting a patch of cedar growing dense and tangled at the base of larger trees, Fargo heaved on the blade. The canoe veered across current, ran through a curtain of droopy branches, and grated to a halt in a shallow. He sprang over the side, seized the bow, and dragged the craft almost entirely from the water as the clamor of chase lifted behind. Quietly gathering his weapons and ammunition, he stood reloading his Colt in the sheltered notch, listening to the noise of raging men rushing downstream.

Loudest was a raucous bellowing: *"Vite! Vite, vous cons, vite!"*

Fargo knew at once whose voice that was. Red Jack Epinard, called Rouge Jacques by the Canucks, chief of Yankee Fur's Fort Providence. And as forms of boats and crew soared by the screening branches, he glimpsed Epinard standing at the foremost bow—

tall and massive in a checked mackinaw, stagged wool trousers, and calked boots, his carroty-red long hair and full beard making it seem like his head was afire.

The big French-Canadian continued shouting abuse at his crew while they charged on down the Okanogan. Then, when the sounds had faded, Fargo launched his canoe and drove once more upriver toward Modoc Doyle's camp.

Just like the old days, he thought with grim sarcasm.

Just like past summers when he'd stabled his horse at Fort Walla Walla and ridden the rivers to a rendezvous with friends he'd not seen for months, even years. He'd not made it very often, but sorely enjoyed the times he had. The annual Doyle's Gather was typical of fur-trade rendezvous where free trappers met with company agents to sell pelts and refit themselves for the coming season. Explorers, hunters, scouts, and other frontiersmen came as well to swap news and lay in supplies, renew ties and feuds, and generally throw a drunken hoorah that could last for weeks. Doyle didn't host it. Nobody ran it. For over a decade now, it would simply happen.

"This's a free-trade jamboree," Modoc Doyle always insisted. "The man that could boss it ain't been born!"

For over a decade now it'd been held at Doyle's, though, for good reason. His encampment, on the Okanogan at the mouth of the Antoine, was conveniently located for those on the Columbia, many of its tributaries, and a number of rivers in British Columbia. Doyle had been one of the first trappers into the Northwest, and as with whores and politicians, age had bestowed respect and honor. Mainly, however, it was because he always had, from some mysterious source, a cache of Thundermug at hand, which could be tapped for a not too unreasonable price.

Thundermug was not merely a whiskey. Its devotees—and they were many—swore it would kill the outlander who tipped it to his lips. They swore with equal enthusiasm that it would cure frostbite, lure the wariest mink into even a clumsily placed trap, and eat the corrosion out of a hopelessly leaded rifle barrel. Fargo himself had found many good friends across a jug of the smoking brew. Modoc Doyle's cache had made his camp the favorite choice.

This year, however, the Trailsman wasn't going to visit and have fun.

It wasn't just like the old days.

It was war.

2

Sunset made a red splash and gave way to darkness. In the thickness of the night, Fargo met the relentless surge of Okanogan current for mile after mile. At long last, with his muscles cramped and arms dead clubs in their sockets, he reached the Antoine, and Modoc Doyle's encampment.

A dozen fires burned in the timber-ringed swale back of the river. Along the bank, a motley assortment of canoes, pirogues, and *bateaux* lay in the grass. Here and there were heaps of roughly baled furs—prime plew from the high valleys of the Northwest. Bearded trappers, long starved for pleasure and social contact, sat about spinning windies and drinking whiskey from horn dippers. Ol' Williams, McHugh, Abel Bone, Renfrew, Toad-eye Topes down from Canada's Similkameen: Fargo was acquainted with many in this strange, wild company of Yanks, Brits, Canucks, Ruskies, 'breeds, and even renegade Indians ousted from their tribes. To most, however, he was a stranger, and not a trapper to boot.

Thus, when Fargo swung out of the dark river and beached his canoe in front of the fires, he aroused immediate suspicion. A couple of trappers came up noiselessly behind him and caught his elbows as he straightened from mooring his canoe. He stabbed quick looks at them on either side of him, but made no defensive move as they led him through the fires. Friends who spotted him hooted and guffawed, his predicament befitting the rowdy joy of a rendezvous, and he grinned to himself. Without leadership, without orders or organization, matters got handled smoothly and decisively, if a mite raucously. If ever the free trappers were to band united . . .

At the center of the shapeless camp, a big-bodied, great-bellied man sat near a whiskey barrel, doling out Thundermug, wearing garments of hide so well greased and worn that he could almost blend chameleonlike with the terrain. His little eyes under shaggy, protruding brows sparked amusedly when the two trappers brought Fargo up to him.

The smaller man announced, "Me an' Vaurien are slipping, Modoc. Down to huntin' two-legged muskrats off the river."

"Like as not a damn spy from the Anglican Company's post at Fort George," the trapper called Vaurien growled, his name and accent indicating a Canuck background. "Let's give him a touch of fire and send him back to his boss."

"Get away from my good pal before he chucks you idiots to the flames," Modoc Doyle retorted, chuckling. "Skye Fargo! By God, I was just sayin' today that I hoped you'd check in before the fur sorting begins. You've been gone a long while. Got to forgive us if we met you with a mite of an edge."

"Too long, Modoc." Fargo hunkered by the flames, accepting a tin cup of whiskey. "There are a lot of new faces here now who couldn't be expected to know me."

"Unfortunately, there're also some of the old faces I don't think will be comin' in this season,"

Doyle replied, sobering. "Appears to be a ruckus brewing between us free traders and the Yankee and Anglican companies. And Quinnalt's band of Klickitat is also prowling, which'll make it even more interesting. Why, right now Red Jack Epinard is six days overdue. He's supposed to come up from Fort Providence to take our furs off our hands. We're stuck here till Epinard shows."

"I'd stick around, too, if I had a couple of bales of plew in these piles," Fargo said, eyeing the stacks appreciatively. "Red Jack's still a Yankee man, I gather, and Yankee's still owned by Ulysses Teague. Teague has a reputation for honesty and fair dealing, even if he does demand his trappers be under contract. But Epinard is all bad. You boys aiming to outfox that fox?"

Doyle shrugged. "Grizzly's more like it when you're talkin' about Red Jack. Us bein' free trappers won't lose Teague no sleep, if our plews end up at Astoria to Yankee credit. But those damn mangy company men, they've tied our heads up neat. Only one other post in the region—Williard Hamilton's Fort George. And Hamilton won't take our trade, period. Either you get a contract with his Anglican Fur Company, or you're a target for every rifle out of Fort Anglican and to hell with your pelts. We're playin' with a striped-back skunk when we deal with Epinard. But it's either that or haul our fur ourselves nigh a thousand miles down to Astoria. Ain't much choice."

"Less choice than you think," Fargo responded grimly, rising and going back to his canoe. Hefting the stiffened body in the bedroll, he returned to Modoc Doyle, startled murmers running ahead of him, and the roistering in the camp stilled. Trappers moved closer, scenting the death he carried, knotting up as they swung in behind while Fargo laid the bedroll on the ground.

"Joel Pegase," he said, pulling aside the folds of the bedroll. "Killed at his own fire, his fur stolen. Whoever did that job left an ambusher to shoot any others voyaging upriver."

Doyle turned ashen. "Who? Who was it?"

Fargo laid the knife with the bloody, beaded haft before Doyle. "That blade says it was Nez Percé. Or rather, now that you mentioned Quinnalt, of a sister tribe like the Klickitat, who'd more likely be around these parts. But it's a good one, too good for an Indian killer to have carelessly left in his victim. It looks to me like a plant." Then Fargo set the Greene capping carbine down. "I pinked the skulker when he tried to pick me off. He dropped this rifle, and I notice it's marked with the star of Yankee Fur."

Alarmed eyes regarded the damning rifle, and above a rumbling discord of trappers, Vaurien snapped at Doyle, "There is your peace. *Sacre bleu!* We've listened too long to your drool about deals, about cooperation, when we should've been answering threats with steel. This settles it!"

"Nothing is settled, Pierre," Doyle retorted, thoroughly shaken. "Might be another plant, to put us at one another's throats. Epinard isn't the only factor that'd spill blood to have furs turn up at Astoria to his credit. But if he's behind it, I'll go after that skunk myself."

"Doubt you'll have to go far," Fargo said acerbically, and relating his pursuit by the Yankee *bateaux*, he concluded, "You mentioned they're overdue, so they weren't coming from here when I saw them heading downriver. Meaning they were on their way here, and turned around either because of the gunshots or the ambusher caught up and warned them. They'll figure out I ditched them pretty soon. I'll bet they've doubled back upriver already, hot

21

on my wake. And believe you me, they were toting war—not trade goods—with them."

Modoc Doyle hunched woodenly for a moment, blinking his eyes and trying to absorb what Fargo had told him. Then he erupted upright into a volcano of roaring action. His great voice lifted over the camp, striking at the scattered groups like a battering ram.

"McHugh," he bellowed, "Hastings, Lanark, Bone! Get a fire going down there on the water. Douse the rest of 'em. If Red Jack Epinard is comin' to burn powder, he needs gettin' burned with some himself."

In seconds, the face of the camp changed. Already many spirits had been dampened by Fargo's gruesome delivery; now the rollicking remainder of boasting, drinking, and even brawling choked off. A grim line was cut across faces that had been stupid with booze or flushed with fun. The bung was slammed back into the whiskey barrel, which was rolled into the brush. Driftwood and logs were dragged swiftly onto the shingle at the water's edge, and a large bonfire was kindled. Fur bales were yanked back to the timber fringe, stacked in one pile, and two men spread out into the grass on either side to guard them. Extra guns were being charged, ramrods whistling in their bores. Doyle himself had plunged down among the boats, flinging men right and left into positions from which they could hamper an attack.

An hour passed.

With the others, Fargo kept straining his eyes downriver. He thought once he detected movement, yet it was too distant and too dark to glimpse any detail. Then it was gone, leaving him with only an unpleasant premonition.

All remained calm.

Fargo grew increasingly apprehensive. The trappers

hadn't come into a rendezvous after a long and bitter winter to wait still, alert against a raid that no one definitely knew would come. Some of them were becoming restive when the swift-skimming shadows of *bateaux* were spotted by one of the trappers patroling the bank.

"Hola, ennemi!" And a moment later, confirming the identity of the approaching crew, "Epinard, Rouge Jacques Epinard!"

A rifle shot drowned out the alarm. A sheet of muzzle flame licked in from the river, and under its cover, the boats swung sharply inward. Among the free trappers' craft, a man spun eerily and fell in the mud. Others broke cover and raced for the camp, preferring to make their stand behind the blazing beacon now flaming high on the riverbank.

Modoc Doyle came loping up, his wide face dripping with sweat, recharging his weapon as he ran. "We're spread too thin," he shouted at Fargo. "They'll come ashore right in the middle of us."

"Spread wider, then," Fargo shot back. "Give them room and let them land, then close fast like jaws on a trap."

Doyle grunted, apparently grateful for someone else's strategy to bolster his own. He wheeled back, roaring to the defenders to give ground, while Fargo sprinted on in a circling loop, searching for some men who could be spared from their present positions. The first of these he saw was a slight, lithe boy hunkering behind a log, laboriously leveling a heavy rifle.

Fargo dropped a quick, hard hand to his shoulder. "Save it for a minute. Trail me. We'll make it hot for them."

The boy glanced up, shook his head. He gestured toward a break of ground closer to the river, where a burly, horse-faced oldster and some of the Canucks were braced against the Yankee men pouring out of the landing *bateaux.*

"I always stick with Papa Brusilov," he protested. "I'll be all right."

"All right!" Fargo pulled up, wheeled back. "Who gives a damn how you'll be?" he snapped. "A kid your age should be as good as a man. Now, damn your hairless chin, get on your hind legs and follow me. We've got a fight to make."

The youth colored, and a blank, half-amused astonishment shone in his eyes. But he straightened, lifted the heavy rifle, and started after Fargo. Circling the camp, Fargo found three more men, two sourdoughs from the Idaho country and the big rawboned Canuck named Vaurien. Swiftly the Trailsman dropped down through the timber and cut out to the river. Swinging upstream again, he brought his little squad within a score of yards of the big fire on the water's edge.

For the first time Fargo got a good look at the attacking force. Forty strong, it was strung out in a double line between the water and the center of the camp, turning its fire two directions against the defenders crouched in the timber on either side. Red Jack Epinard was about midway up the line of his men, watching for a chance to work across to the stack of baled furs. Fargo dropped those with him into the thick grass and paused. Directly those defenders who were with Papa Brusilov in the little break of ground were caught in a crossfire and forced to drop back. When they did this, Epinard shouted and a party broke for the fur bales.

Fargo turned to his squad then. "Cut loose," he ordered tersely. "Start at the river. Pick every man off in that double line that you can. Work slow and work sure. Epinard's boys won't like lead in their backs any better than we do, and we might turn them!"

They opened up, their weapons roaring, flaming into the night, as they desperately tried to stop the yelling, shooting attackers who were rushing the bales of fur. Fargo concentrated on three who suddenly veered aside in a flanking maneuver. He hit the first in the breastbone, the second when he turned, hesitating, and the third in his lower back while he was fleeing back to the main force. Then, rolling on his side to reload, he glanced over to see how the others were faring, and saw that the boy with the big rifle was having trouble with its weight. Dropping his revolver and some ammo beside the slim figure, he lifted the rifle.

"Here, you reload for us. We'll make a fighter out of you yet."

The boy cast a quick, venomous glance at him.

Fargo laughed and picked off a Fort Providence raider who was swinging a gun butt at one of the guards beside the fur bales.

For some reason, Vaurien took offense and intervened, snarling. "Stick to your shooting, *mon ami*, and leave the *enfant* alone, or Papa Brusilov will close your fat mouth with steel."

The youth shoved Fargo's revolver back, fully reloaded now, his lips curling above even teeth. "Mind your own shooting, Pierre Vaurien. You're doing little of it."

Fargo's grin widened at the scowl that darkened the Canuck's face, but the youth ignored both men, reaching for a spent rifle and plumbing its bore with a practiced stab of its rod. As he retrieved his revolver, though, Fargo's grin froze. Despite the determined fire pouring out of the grass into the backs of Epinard's crew, the Fort Yankee boss had gotten half a dozen of his men among the piled furs. They were pawing hurriedly for the choicest bales, while the way back to the boats was held open by the still-unbroken double line of men. Worse, another little party was bucketing water out of the river over the huge beacon Doyle had ordered lit on the bank. The fire was guttering low, robbing the flame-stabbed darkness of the camp of its last light.

Yelling a sharp command to keep the gunfire coming from where his band crouched, Fargo leapt up and sprinted away. More than once free trappers shot at him, unable to tell friend from foe in the gloomy melee, but it was hard shooting and the slugs went wide. The Trailsman drove straight at where he had last spied Epinard, hoping to take the leader and break the back of the attack. But Epinard had moved in the murk and at least temporarily was lost from Fargo's view. He turned a little and charged toward the raiders at the fur bales, while across the camp somebody else had the same notion. Modoc Doyle's bull-roarer voice thundered into the night.

"At 'em, lads! We got hides to skin!"

It was a grim, heartening call, but it was answered by an equally loud cry from Epinard rallying his forces: "*Guerre à mort!*" Following the shout, Fargo glimpsed Epinard now, just as Red Jack leapt at a trapper. The trapper made a frantic stab for his knife, but Epinard ripped out his throat with a lightning stroke of his *poignard,* and the other man sank, fountaining blood.

Again Fargo charged toward Epinard, only to have a raider blunder into him with a fur bale across his shoulders. Fargo kicked his feet out from under him, sledged the top of his head with his gun butt, and ran on. A pistol spewed flame almost into his face, blinding him for a moment, but he caught one of the shooter's arms. Jerking the arm across the top of his shoulder, he wheeled and bent double, throwing the leverage of his body against the arm. Bone snapped and the man sailed limply over Fargo's head.

Down by the river a new alarm broke.

"They're headin' for the water."

Angling back toward the river at a full run, Fargo crashed into another running figure. Still focusing on Epinard, but unable to make out faces in the darkness, Fargo sank fingers into a man's shoulders. The man turned like a huge bobcat, swinging a hard fist into Fargo's face. It rattled his teeth and he went down, but he pulled the man with him. Furiously Fargo rolled on the grass, trying to get clear, and when the other's bulk pressed against him, he set his hard-muscled legs about the middle of his opponent in a merciless scissors grip.

They lay together silently, their breath whistling, one resisting a deadly grip, the other trying to bring it into full play. Down by the river Fargo heard firing build rapidly, then come to an abrupt halt. A harsh, angry shout raised up along the water.

"Them mangy cutthroats! They're gettin' away!"

The man under Fargo rolled against the scissors in a great, straining effort that gave him a moment's breath before the savage grip shifted expertly and closed again. "Not all of 'em," the man wheezed desperately. "Give a hand here, quick! I've got one o' the devils."

With a grunt Fargo broke his hold and sat up. Something tugged at him with the sound of the man's half-boastful, half-pleading cry—something that had to get out of him before it split him wide open. His laughs echoed against the timber.

"Fargo," Doyle snorted painfully from a yard away. "You! Damn you for a belly-bustin' bullsnake. Ain't a whole rib left in my carcass."

3

By newly kindled fires a stock of the damage was taken.

Scarcely a man escaped numerous scratches, contusions, sprains, and cuts, and there were plenty of broken limbs, smashed faces, and bullet and knife wounds to go around. A count of the furs showed Epinard's raiders had swiped three bales of prime plew, but not without cost: a tally of the dead showed he had lost eleven men to four from the rendezvous. That, and knowing the Fort Providence crew had been twice as strong as their own, drew some of the sting from the attack.

It mollified Modoc Doyle not at all, it seemed. He rubbed at his ribs and cussed foully at Skye Fargo, yet there was a glint of high fun in the old trapper's eyes that belied the blackness of his countenance.

The same glint was in Papa Brusilov's onyx eyes when he led the kid Fargo had drafted last night across to where the Trailsman was sitting. Up close, Fargo estimated Brusilov was in his early sixties, his blocky muscular body down but not out, though his shoulders were slightly stooped. His gray-whiskered horse face was topped by sparse gray hair neatly plastered to his skull, and when he spoke, it was with a guttural Russian accent right off the steppes.

"*Dziekuje*—thanks," Brusilov said solemnly. "Papa Olaf owes you a great something. For t'ree year I haff take care of this li'l one, here. For t'ree year I haff try to do what nature haff make impossible, to make a Cossack of this one. But you!" Turning to the rest of the trappers, Brusilov raised his voice roguishly. "Comrades, what a woods-runner this one is. In a single night, he make a man of Natasha. My Netty swears that now she is a man, by gar."

Fargo stared at the kid. The more he stared, the more he saw how nitwit blind he'd been. This was a girl facing him! Slim and nubile, she was, with the devil in her dark eyes, a man's shirt loosely covering her pert breasts, a man's denims cupping her boyish rump, and her raven-black hair rolled tight to fit under her knitted *voyageur* cap.

He felt heat flood his face. He saw the frown wash from Doyle's jaw. The old trapper burst into roaring laughter that paid Fargo back in full for his own humor at having bent Doyle's ribs in the dark. Alone of all those in the camp, the girl didn't laugh. But the mischievous, taunting little smile on her lips was harder to bear than the howls of the trappers. Stung, he rose to his feet and cast Doyle a cool eye, asking evenly, "Okay, okay, what now?"

Before Doyle could scrub the tears from his eyes and respond, Pierre Vaurien jeered scornfully, "What else, but fight to get our plew back from those Fort Providence pirates. Most of us will, anyhow. A few may think to get our pelts back like they try to get peace, by begging, *non?*"

Some of the gathered trappers chorused their support, suggesting vengeful plans, but the majority gave out a hushed gasp at the Canuck's unsubtle derision of Modoc Doyle. And Doyle, sobering fast, nailed Vaurien with resentful eyes, his voice a hard, frigid rasp.

"Point out them few, if you dare. I see no cowards, only the bravest men on the rivers. Smart, too. Everyone here lives by producing pelts and knows that unless there's peace, there'll be death for many and profits for none."

"Bah! We know of men vanishing, caches looted," Vaurien argued, stabbing with a thick forefinger. "We see that even as trader bosses listened to you plead for peace, they were plotting to rob and kill."

"Okay, perhaps I failed. Perhaps heads of fur companies ain't got ears for free trappers. Maybe someone other'n a trapper, such as Skye here, would've gotten further, learned more, maybe still could." Doyle, pausing for emphasis, nodded at Fargo. "I won't deny Red Jack Epinard's playin' dirty and has to be laid low. But as hard as we've had it from them companies, they've never been this scurvy. It's tough to believe the top gents like Teague and Hamilton would try such low-down tricks. I'm not saying not. I'm saying let's try to find out before we strike."

Hearing this, Fargo realized why Doyle wanted him to come here. It wasn't to make war. He'd fought, and would probably have to keep fighting, but these buckos didn't need to import talent. Nope, he'd been called up to make peace. Apparently Doyle assumed the others involved in this clash also knew and trusted Fargo, and they'd welcome his just opinion as neither trapper nor company agent. Well, some he'd known too well, and some he'd met at one time or another, and none would tolerate meddling, he bet. Most likely they'd distrust him double, which was fair, because he sure didn't trust any of them.

The same kind of suspicious rancor seemed to be splitting the camp, Fargo realized. Toad-eye, Abel

Bone, all the old regulars who'd been coming here since its inception, were grouping about one fire with some of the newer bunch like Papa Brusilov and Natasha. Vaurien was drawing the Canucks, the 'breeds, and Iron Hat, the renegade Paiute, toward the scattered fur pile.

At the fire, a man was declaring, "Worthy a try, it is, snoopin' an' hagglin' instead of wastin' blood. Aye, when it comes down to it, assailin' the devil we know is better'n a devil we don't."

"A waste of time! It won't work," one of the half-breeds scoffed. "We'll lose weeks, the pelts too."

"Whatever we do, we'll need a place we can work from," Fargo said thoughtfully. "A camp where we can mold bullets and stack furs without getting raided like tonight. While you men settle in, I'll voyage east up the Columbia to Fort George at Kettle Falls. If we're aiming to tackle Epinard, it'd be nice to know Hamilton wouldn't sic his Anglican Fur crew on us when we were spread thin."

"Parley? *Incroyable!* They understand only two things: the gun and the knife! But Pierre, he understands them, and I understand you too, outlander!" Vaurien raged at Fargo, then turned to rant at Doyle. "For long time I think you are getting old. Too old for smart trapper. *Certainement!* This is proof. You believe this Fargo like he is our brother. He could be Anglican Fur spy, making trap. Could be spy for Rouge Jacques Epinard also!"

Doyle rose, seeming to have grown to greater girth and stature under the tirade. "I'll vouch for Skye, so will others. Don't be stupid!"

"It is too late for that. We are *fini!* The fur, she is scattered from the bale, and no one can tell which belong to him or how much. I take my men and they take one-half of fur. More easy than counting, *hein?*"

31

"Half!" Doyle roared. "You stinkin' coyote, you an' them white bellies all together never added up to a quarter of that stack. Damn you, Vaurien. For ten seasons the free trade's stuck together, and because we did, we've made our way. You know that. Now, when we're against our roughest haul, you slide out. I'd see you in hell before you grab off half that plew."

A flinty grin creased the Canuck's face as his hand, whipping to the back of his neck, returned with a curve-bladed skinner knife. He thrust the steel forward till the point pressed against the swell of Doyle's belly. "Stand easy. The knife is sharp and the hand is quick. I aimed to play fair, but now I am a coyote. A coyote don't care what he scavenge. So, we take all the fur, and if there is a fight, Modoc die—so!"

He made a short, ugly motion of the knife, which, if it had been shoved deep, would have disemboweled the rotund trapper. Doyle's face went white. Ol' Williams and Lanarck and the others stood like graven granite, careful that they didn't startle the rebel Canuck into plunging his blade to the hilt. Papa Brusilov, his intense eyes molten with anger, trembled as he held his hands protectively on Natasha's shoulders. Vaurien's companions hastily loaded themselves with fur and started for the boats. It was too much for the headstrong Natasha to swallow; twisting from Brusilov's paternal hold, she impulsively flung herself at Vaurien, cursing him luridly.

"Such language! I shall wash your mouth out with . . . something," Vaurien chortled, catching Natasha with his free hand. "*Viens dans mes bras*—come into my arms," he said, and pulled her close, ignoring the flailing of her fists.

"Take your dirty hands off Netty," Brusilov commanded, infuriated to recklessness. "She's not for your kind; she's a lady!"

"*Oui, oui!*" Vaurien took no offense, and neither did he take warning. "A beautiful lady, *mon vieux*." His thick arm went about the girl. "She will be the queen of the squaws in our camp, cooking my food, binding my wounds, and gladdening my eye."

Squirming madly, Natasha sank her teeth into Vaurien's arm. With a sharp, angry oath, he tried to shake her loose, but she clamped to his wrist with a tenacious jaw hold, until he finally wrenched her brutally free.

It happened in a moment, but it was the tiny break in the Canuck's attention that Fargo needed. He could have drawn and shot Vaurien, he supposed, but killing the damn fool was a mite drastic. Trying to wound was too risky; he couldn't aim fast enough, and if he missed, he might hit someone else and Vaurien might hit him. Besides, it all seemed too simple, not enough of a lasting impression. So instead Fargo surged in, caught the rawboned Canuck by the shoulder, and when Vaurien spun to stab him, he knocked the skinner knife aside and punched Vaurien square in the mouth of his rage-crimsoned face.

Spraying blood and teeth, Vaurien hurtled backward and tripped, falling over a stump. Fargo kicked the knife back out of the way and started forward. Vaurien came up explosively, charging, the knuckles of his left hand grazing Fargo's temple as he slid past. Then Fargo locked both his own hands together, raised them over his head, and brought them down in a crushing blow upon the nape of the neck as Vaurien tore by, and the Canuck dropped sprawling facedown in the dirt.

Fargo leapt on top of him, got a grip on his ears, and banged his face into the hard ground. Vaurien squirmed around savagely, unseated his tormentor, then flung himself full upon Fargo, who was waiting for him. Instead of Fargo's chest, Vaurien struck the soles of the Trailsman's upraised boots. With a violent spring of his legs, Fargo sent the big Canuck arching away from him.

Both men rose together. Vaurien rushed at Fargo, out to maim him for life, his intention clear in his hooded eyes as he struck Fargo a glancing blow to the side of the face, only to take a sharp counter to the jaw in return. He pivoted, leading with a loopy right. Fargo slid under it and drove his own left deep into Vaurien's belly. Vaurien gasped in pain and immediately reached for Fargo with his long arms. Fargo backed away, not wishing to be trapped in that fashion, but a roundhouse swing that he failed to elude caught him high on the head and knocked him off his feet.

There was an immediate roar from the throng of onlookers, who didn't give a damn who won or why, just so long as the bout was a ripsnorter. Fargo felt as if his head had been torn from his shoulders; rarely in all his brawling days had he encountered a man who could punch like Vaurien. He got up because to stay down meant being trampled under Vaurien's boots. But his vision was blurred and he shuffled a bit as he backed away, trying to marshal his strength.

Vaurien followed, smirking. "*Bon voyage, crétin,*" he said, and moved in for the kill.

Without warning Fargo stopped retreating. Vaurien kept coming; he charged Fargo with a long right that missed, followed it with another right, and Fargo, weaving, slammed a left hook into his midsection. Vaurien wretched on the spot, and as he doubled over in pain, Fargo snapped him upright again with a bruising uppercut. The Canuck reeled backward, windmilling, struck a log, and tumbled into a haphazard pile of firewood. A jagged sliver of broken pine skewered his side. He bellowed in mingled pain and rage, tore it out of his flesh, and started to get up, the sharp-edged shard of wood held in his hand like a dagger.

He was rising from his knees when Fargo barged in, smashing him on his pulpy mouth with a hammering right. Vaurien flipped over backward, losing his crude weapon. Fargo didn't wait for Vaurien to rise again. He came in fast while the Canuck was trying to get clear of the wood debris, lashed out twice to Vaurien's belly, then lifted his fists and slammed the trapper's face askew. A short, sledging right ended the fight before Vaurien had time to raise a fist.

Fargo stepped back and let Vaurien cling to the logs, sobbing breath back into his tortured body, but only for a brief moment. Then he placed a solid grip on Vaurien and began frog-marching him ignominiously toward the boats.

By now Abel Bone and Renfrew had their revolvers up, trained stonily on the Canuck's crew. Bales of fur spilled from nerveless shoulders. In moments the whole party was at the edge of the water.

"Bon voyage," Fargo told Vaurien, shoving him forward.

The Canuck whimpered. "But the plew. One-quarter belongs to us."

"Bon voyage!" The words were as brittle as shattered ice.

Vaurien stood uncertainly for a moment, his eyes blazing and the pain of his beating pulling his face into a grotesque mask of hatred. Then he turned and stepped into the *bateau*. "I teach you more French," he said between the stumps of his teeth. "I teach you much when we meet again."

Fargo tried to tell himself that the rendezvous was well rid of Pierre Vaurien, that the trapper had reaped only what he had sowed. But as he stared at the departing craft, he sensed that someday he would be learning more French, as surely as the rise of tomorrow's sun. And the lesson would be bitter.

Alongside Fargo on the bank, Modoc Doyle waited quietly. When at last Vaurien and his maverick crew were lost in the shadows down the river, Doyle turned and touched Fargo's arm. "Thanks, Skye. Vaurien's a blowhard with emphasis on hard. He shoves, but he sure can't stomach bein' shoved. He's been needin' his sails trimmed for a while now. Ain't sorry we got rid o' the other grouchers with him, either. Everyone here now'll stick by us, I reckon."

Fargo nodded slackly. He stood, legs spread, feet planted in the dirt, his clothes and flesh begrimed, his chest still heaving from his recent exertions. His voice was dull, weary. "You work a crew up any way you think best, and let's try to hit on a good hideout tonight. Sooner the better—on that, at least, Vaurien wasn't spouting windies."

When they turned back into the camp, they saw Natasha seated hunkering over the fire, one hand up to a bruise across one cheek. A torrid flame burned in her eyes. But it was no match for the consuming heat in those of Papa Brusilov, crouched in awkward comfort beside her. Glancing up as Fargo and Doyle approached, he growled his wrath like a vindictive grizzly.

"I come from Novo Arkhangelsk of the far nort'. I am Russe, also once I am priest till I sicken in head. I cast off my cloth, t'row away the book, and come here because I am *plokhóy*—bad, a demon. Then I find her one Christmas, so I call her my Noël child, Natasha. She heal me, make me good again." Pausing, Brusilov glanced wildly about. "Is insult to Netty, Olaf, Russe, to life. That Canuck eunuch! He soil my *krásivyi tsvetok*—beautiful flower, he hurt her. I vow I hurt him. With my bare hands, very slow, I kill him one soon day!''

"Papa! Hush!" Natasha scolded, yet a gentleness in her voice seemed to wilt the tempest in Brusilov.

He slumped back, chastened, as Fargo swept the girl with an appraising glance. Close up now, bathed by firelight, she appeared more mature than before, perhaps in her early twenties, her features a coy blend of frail innocence and firm experience: mouth wide and stubborn, a nose angled at a delicate tilt. Again her depthless black eyes arrested Fargo, challenging him when she caught his notice of her.

"Checking my pelt?" she teased. "I'm not one of the furs you just cheated Pierre Vaurien out of."

Fargo shrugged. "The only hide I got off him was his own, Netty, eh, Natasha."

"Netty will do, Mr. Fargo. But you did keep Vaurien's share."

"Skye will do." He smiled. "We'll store the furs until the troubles past, then divvy them up—"

"Like all good thieves?" Natasha flashed an impudent grin. "There are going to be a lot of people looking for us. Epinard and his Yankee crew, Hamilton and all his Anglican men, and now Vaurien if he can escape the others—and Papa. You were right when you said we'd need a hideout. We'll show you one."

Olaf Brusilov rumbled reprovingly, but Natasha waved away his opposition. "I know it's a risk, Papa. So's everything else, and you won't make me no safer if you don't give our friends shelter. A priest always gives sanctuary. In the morning we can lead everyone to our home, our Zashcíta!"

4

The next two days were spent journeying to Natasha's haven.

Presumably if conditions and luck were fair—as they were—the distance could have been covered in a single, exhaustively long day. But on that first morning, by time the hungover trappers got packed and launched, such a push was too late to attempt. The men weren't in a great hurry anyhow, preferring to travel by daylight, then pulling their boats high and dry and relaxing all night.

For once Fargo didn't have to break trail, and he enjoyed the luxury of running with the pack while others guided. The trappers were still in a rambunctious mood, prone to sailing three sheets to the wind while belting out songs in spiritous baritones. It made no difference that the songs and the tongues in which they were sung came from distant foreign lands. Their voices were as one native to this region, catching the rush of white water, thunder in high peaks, the soughs of promised summer across Pacific Northwest valleys.

En route, Fargo chanced to learn that the hideaway's name, Zashcíta, was Russian for "shelter." Indeed it was, a small, concealed canyon formed by an accident of geology and erosion and the Nespelem River. The Nespelem had its beginnings somewhere in the heart of the northern Colville range, and squirreling south, the little river had found its passage blocked by the sharp, unbroken rise of the last ridge between itself and the Columbia River. Searching with the persistence of water, it had located a crevasse and had cut an underground conduit through the ridge. On the Columbia side it jetted out of solid rock like a huge spring. What Natasha and Brusilov had discovered was that in some previous age, the Nespelem had cut another underground channel beneath the ridge, then had abandoned it for the one it now used. There was, then, a few rods from where the river burst from the rock cliff, a brush-covered hole that was the mouth of a tunnel: the old, waterworn channel leading under the front peaks to the shelter of Zashcíta.

The floor of the pocket was bowl-shaped, flourishing with tall grass, scrub, and thickets of aspen, fir, and pine. Near the channel orifice in the pocket wall, a rather long and narrow spring-fed pool bordered a wide, flat clearing. Toward the rear of the clearing was a cabin of weathered boards, with a chimney that looked like a pile of rocks, and a roof that slanted down to form a lean-to in back. A footpath curved from the cabin and worked up the pocket wall to a pinnacle on the front rim, from which a vista of mountains, the Nespelem basin, and the great Columbia spread out into the haze of distance. The path did not continue, nor were there any other connecting trails; the steep sides of the pocket and the surrounding chain of tall ridges made entry nigh on impossible except by way of the channel. This was truly a shelter, to which battle-scarred men could retreat and recover.

Or throw a binge.

On the evening of their arrival, the trappers pitched

camps out about the bowl, leaving the cabin to Brusilov and Natasha. That was just as well, since the earthen-floored interior was cramped and murky, with built-in bunks hemming the sides, and the stone fireplace bulging over most of the rear wall. They swarmed inside, though, when Natasha was collecting foodstuffs for a potluck, and again later as they shared in her resultant mulligatawny stew. Otherwise they stayed afield, where she could join 'em or avoid 'em as she chose, while they guzzled and cracked heads, wind, and kegs of whiskey. The rendezvous was back on, with nary a belch lost in the move.

It irritated Fargo, on two counts.

The trappers got to whoop; they didn't have to go anywhere tomorrow. He did. And to leave at dawn, all set, he had to get ready tonight. As he headed from the gathering, he eyed them swilling Thundermug, swapping yarns, and lying owlishly, and felt a pang of regret. But this was not his night to howl.

Set off from the main cluster of campsites, his camp consisted of a bedroll and the supplies from the canoe. To take only this trip's needs required he tediously sort and repack everything, and to break the monotony, he carried out each container as it was completed. On way to the tunnel, he could scan the campfires crackling merrily, their flames casting a ruby glow up the walls and piercing the darkness that hemmed the pocket rim. From over at the river, where Fargo exited the tunnel, that fiery reflection was seen as hovering low glow against the upper ridgeline, intensifying the ominousness of the black clouds scudding above ridge of rock.

The clouds flowed by in clumps, and when overhead, they blocked the moon's light. One batch caught Fargo within the brushy copses flanking the river, where he was dragging his canoe out to the bank.

"Too damn dark to piss, even," Fargo grumbled, hardly exaggerating, for the clouds had plunged night into coal-pit black.

He stayed put, chary of putting a foot through a trapper's boat, cussing the clouds and wondering if they portended stormy weather. When it was merely night again, he ported his canoe out around to where the river was close by the tunnel mouth. Cleared of clouds, the sky was a velvet backdrop for an ivory half-moon and an impressive, if cold, diamond spray of stars. Together, their vapid glows were sufficiently brilliant to bathe the flat, open space where the Trailsman slowly, methodically inspected his canoe.

By now Fargo had carted out almost all of the trip supplies, stashing them in the riverbank foliage. The tunnel had proved slippery and devious, its passage streaming seepages and backup water. It took two full dunkings, never mind slips, for Fargo to wise up and strip to his trousers. His sodden shirt, boots, and other garb were here also, hanging to dry. Now, scrutinizing his canoe's seamed, membrane hide, his eye caught a number of small cuts, tears, and deep scuffs that needed attending. From a container he took gut, needle, an awl, and other simple tools and supports, then settled in sewing for a while.

The river area was placidly silent, and at times snatches of revelry would echo hollowly through the tunnel or filter down from the glowing rim of the pocket. Earlier the rendezvous had vexed him on two counts; but one, regret at missing it, had long since faded. The other lingered, too slight to pursue, yet pesky as a saddle burr. Concern, that's what it was; that sort of on-edge feeling any wary man gets when things weren't up to snuff. And to his style of thought, it was incautious to resume the rendezvous, even reckless and foolhardy not to post a lookout or patrol the tunnel's river frontage. Yet Fargo couldn't fault the trappers. By nature they were brash, confident of their prowess. They had no fear of attack. They were accustomed to the virulence of fur companies and the occasional malice of roving Indians, and not for such things would any man of them forgo an hour of carousing. And yet . . .

Over the period Fargo had been passing in and out of the pocket, he sensed that growing uneasiness sat with the trappers around the fires. They were ripping, but their roar was sounding muted to him, subdued by memories, tempered by worries, earnest talk dampening ardent blarney. The rendezvous would be on a roll for some time yet, but he suspected it would halt when it ran out of booze or into morning, whichever struck first. Either one would have a sobering impact.

Almost done with his repairs, Fargo was feeling a simple contentment in the sewing, a certain pride in a skill well done. If it weren't for where he was, and why he was here, and some rising worries about a canyon full of dipsy trappers, he would have been happy. Well, until he returned to Zashcíta, he figured, at least he'd have some peace and contentment out here.

He figured wrong.

Natasha came drifting out of the tunnel. She had changed clothes, into the same sort of pants and an old-style immigrant laborer shirt that laced up the front. Another singular difference was that they were soaking wet. She wasn't wearing her knit cap, and the sheen of moonglow showed that her hair was wet. Her eyes were wet too, and her cheeks flushed, looking almost rouged. Obviously she'd fallen coming through the tunnel; as an expert in that endeavor, Fargo knew all the signs.

"Food for your trip," she called, holding up a bulky parcel wrapped in paper and string.

Glad to have the food and know why she came here, Fargo thanked Natasha, watching her trim body hastening like an eager promise. She was young—not that young, but young enough to brim with gamine vitality while exuding a sort of vixenish appeal that stoked older notions in his mind. He knew those signs, too, though no sane man would claim expertise on women. And heeding his own signs, he turned to finish his canoe before those errant notions became physically evident.

Approaching, Natasha put the parcel by a tree, then came close to watch mutely while Fargo worked. After a few moments she began to unlace her shirt-front, tugging slowly, abstractedly, still gazing silently. Not till Fargo completed and moved the canoe to a safer spot, did she speak, remarking quite casually, "Lord, I'm still so damp!" She pulled the open front of her shirt away from skin that was the color and texture of cream. "That's better," she sighed, smiling unabashed. "Sit down. Rest, Skye."

"No, I've my tools to pack away."

"No!" Laughing, she grabbed his arm. The way her shirtfront fell away from her scarcely concealed breasts made her look particularly wanton. "You know, I never did thank you properly for what you did to Vaurien."

"No thanks necessary," Fargo replied gruffly. He could feel the heat, the sexual sparring that was building between them. How much of hers was flirting and how much was passion, he couldn't tell, and didn't think much mattered. It was the prurient surging in his own loins, *that's* what he was trying to resist, and not for Natasha's sake, either. Another time, another place, he'd have flattened her to the nearest bed without hesitation . . . but here? A tunnel away was her adopted father and a throng of protective uncles, the lot of them cockeyed on tiger milk. If a trapper staggered outside . . . if she so much as peeped that he'd pressed advances on their darlin' child and sweetheart mascot . . . Well, if he weren't mangled by Brusilov, he'd be skinned alive. Or worse. Trapped into marriage. The thought chilled his brain, but no such sensible effect was occurring down below where he needed it. Rather the reverse; the wrong resolve was stiffening. He could feel himself hardening against his will, and he tried to shift, his beginning erection bulging out the crotch of his pants.

So Fargo moved. Then Natasha moved, clinging gently to his midriff while easing in to face him, and he could feel her warm breath against his cheek and smell the fragrance of her cleansed skin as she pressed close, murmuring, "I never could've gotten away from that brute, Skye, never by myself. And this is how I want to thank you."

She kissed him. Fargo felt her arms glide up and tighten around him, and a responsive swelling in his traitorous groin. After a moment of her torrid, tight kiss, he broke off, trying to hold her at bay as he said, "Fine. Now you've thanked me."

"Not enough." And she kissed him again, lazily, sensuously, her hands flat on his bare chest. This time she broke it off, but only to move her lips to his ear, a breast squeezing against him as she leaned up, a plaintive whimpering sound to her voice. "Am I so gruesome from what Vaurien did that you don't want me?"

"No, no, you're beautiful, lumps and all. But you're—"

"Not good enough?" She nibbled his ear, her fingers stroking his bare flesh. "Do you think I'm worn out," she whispered, "from too many men?"

"Oh, no, just the opposite."

"Then I'm a mere babe to you?" She brushed her

lips and the pink tip of her tongue teasingly across his mouth, her hand sliding to his waist as she did so. "Do you think you'd be robbing the cradle?"

It was almost impossible for Fargo to keep from touching her. Natasha was getting a rise out of him, no denial, but a part of him still wanted to hold out, if only because she'd been working so diligently at it and he felt slightly manipulated. She knew signs too, he was sure, and probably had dreamed up a few variations herself in her short time. Replying to her question, he began to protest, "You're grown . . ." when he suddenly hitched in his breath, his blood pounding as he heard her coo. "Not like you, Skye." All this while, her curious fingers had been moving along the bulge in his groin, traveling its length. "You're very grown . . ."

At that point, it *was* impossible.

Fargo caught her by both shoulders and returned her kiss. Natasha glued her mouth to his, eyes closed, nostrils quivering. His lips shifted from her mouth to her throat, and then she stopped him, breaking away. She faced him with eyes curiously tight across the corners, and waited, silent.

Fargo knew what for. Slowly he eased off her shirt, then one by one stripped her of garments, using the shirt to caressingly daub her naked flesh, as though it were a towel and he was drying her after a bath. He dried her from neck to feet, and she didn't stir, except to cup her breasts. They weren't small and they weren't udders, either, though her hands couldn't quite contain them; they were firm, so firm that they stood out from her like fleshy cones. When she pushed their tautened nipples out, Fargo could see, too, the quivering ripple of arousal along her stomach muscles. Her tummy was flat; she didn't have to tuck it in. Her waist went in, though not so as to divide her body into an hourglass; while definitely female, her hips weren't that broad. Her pudenda was plump, with fleshy lips and black hair—delicate and dark, just a thin line of velvety curls spearing an accent mark along her cleft, drawing Fargo's attention like steel filings to a lodestone.

As Fargo finished drying her, she leaned close, whispering quickly, her mouth so near he could taste the sweetness of it. "Not here, Skye. I mean, who knows who'd pop from the tunnel or on the river?" Gripping his arm then, she began gliding quickly into the bordering strip of tree and brush. And Fargo stayed right alongside, wondering why the hell he was allowing himself to get into this. Natasha didn't have her clothes on, maybe, but she was coming with too many strings attached to be naked, and he needed trouble like a case of ringworm. Well, the reason was simple; he answered his own question—Natasha didn't have her clothes on.

Natasha stepped a pace more, just enough to conceal them in the overhanging copse. Her eyes aglow with hidden fires, she unsnapped his belt and popped the top button, Fargo sensing she was hot with anticipation as she unbuttoned his fly and tugged his pants down, removing them and his boots. He drew her up straight against him then and gently lowered them in an embrace onto a bed of leaves and springy grasses. His hands moved compulsively, spreading tenderly across her flat belly and up over her taut breasts. He could feel her trembling from his touch, and warmth flowed through him, warmth as downy as the texture of her skin.

Natasha shuddered and gripped him by the waist, urging his hand to slide between her legs and upward along her sleek inner thighs. Her hips slackened, widening to allow him access while she kept murmuring in a low passionate voice, "I want you, I want you . . . Take me, take me, fill me up . . ."

His hand slid down, down. Caressing fingertips

reveled in the softness of her appreciative body, slithering into the lightly haired puff that creased her mound. She moaned, arching her hips, and used both hands to grasp and massage the exposed shaft of his erection. In turn, his hand slid up and down, up and down, gently and slowly, just the tips of his fingers caressing the pursed seam of her nether lips. Natasha opened and closed her eyes, gasping and whimpering. Her buttocks jerked and quivered, her legs rolling and squirming, heels digging into the earth.

"Don't tease me, Skye," she mewled, panting harshly. "Put it in, oh, please, please put it in." In a frenzy, she splayed her legs wider to cradle him between them, one hand urging him over her, the other reaching between and guiding his taunting member against the opening of her moist sheath. "Now," she sighed breathlessly. "Damn you, now . . ."

Fargo could feel her young body throbbing as she slowly undulated beneath him. Prodding him into herself with her now trembling fingers, Natasha began to absorb him, moaning, wincing a little, yet greedy for more. "Ah, God, you are Peter the Great. You must be. Peter the Great . . ."

Fargo, tensing downward, felt the gripping of her loins tearing at his entrails, and he clasped her waist and penetrated deeper, the whole of him inside her small belly as she arched her back off the ground. Her nubile thighs pressed against his legs as her ankles snaked over and locked around his calves. Fargo could feel her eager young muscles tightening smoothly around him while he pumped deep into her soft, willing flesh. She strained under him, moaning with his thrusts, opening and closing her thighs, her head thrashing from side to side in total abandon. He could feel himself still growing and expanding inside her youthfully tight sheath until he felt as if he were going to explode from the exquisite pleasure building within him.

"More! Yes! More!" Natasha pleaded, urging Fargo on with the pounding of her heels high on his legs. He struggled to comply, pistoning into her with deeper and faster strokes. Tighter wrapped her limbs, deeper sank her fingernails, rhythmically matching Fargo's building tempo while his pent-up orgasm flared up boiling, on the verge of eruption.

She pushed against him, squeezing harder as she sensed his imminent release. Shivering uncontrollably, she cried out as Fargo spurted violently into her, then shuddered convulsively with the impact of her responding climax. Her petite body undulated, then collapsed limply, and she was still, save for the uncontainable quivering of her thighs pressed firmly against his flanks. They both lay quiet, satiated.

Presently, with a deep sigh, Fargo withdrew and eased off to stretch languidly alongside Natasha. Finally she stirred and caressed his cheek.

"Guess I should say thanks again, Skye. Well, I do say it." Slowly she swung up to sit cross-legged on the grass. 'This doesn't happen very often to me, Skye."

"Well, happens to all of us at one time or another."

"It's not supposed to happen at all." She paused, her expression becoming querulously troubled. "I . . . I have a sexual fever, Skye. I'll be perfectly fine, a good girl, and then something, somebody triggers the fever. Passion rises in me, consuming, that seems to snap inside, like the spring of an old watch. Bang, thataway." As she spoke, her fingers were wandering around his chest and abdomen, seeming to gravitate of their own volition lower in sweeping circles to his belly and loins. After a long sigh, she added, "Don't worry, Skye. I blame myself, not you."

"It's nobody's fault. Maybe it just happened, is

all, you can always say that. Me, I think we should take credit, not blame. We got rewarded."

She looked disgusted. "Just goes to show you don't know much about women."

"That's something I've never claimed," Fargo replied with a laugh, which changed pitch abruptly as he felt her hand stray to his genitals. By all rights he should have no interest or ability down there, but some strong tinglings were already flowing through his flaccid shaft. He tried to smile reassuringly at Natasha, but his usual attempts at such niceties made him look like a lopsided lobo, and just about as trustworthy. He tried to think of what he might say, which wasn't one of his talents, either. "Well, Netty, stop whipping yourself. I do know that passion and desire don't make anyone feel sick or guilty. Only the hate and resentment that can be hidden in them cause sickness and bitter regrets."

"I don't know about that, Skye. I just know what happens to me, my sudden feeling out of nowhere, overwhelming me for God knows how long. I wanted to tell you, had to tell you." Natasha smiled, first tentatively, then fully, and leaned against his chest. "So you'll know what to expect, Skye. The unexpected. Only fair to warn you, and get what I feel worked out straight between us."

Fargo glanced down at his crotch. Then Natasha looked, her eyes smoky and hungry as she stared at his rapidly reviving erection.

"Netty," Fargo said, "you have definitely done that. What you're feeling you've worked out straight between us."

5

Dawn was a pale, cloud-opaque gray laced with pink when Skye Fargo arose and prepared to leave for Fort George.

Around him, the pocket reverberated with the besotted snores of trappers sleeping off their toot. A stubborn few, though, were hanging awake to the last swallow, among them Modoc Doyle, who wobbled over to bid Fargo good-bye and good luck. No mention was made of Natasha, no query as to her whereabouts last night. Fargo was relieved; he and Natasha had taken care when slipping back into camp, but couldn't be sure they'd not been observed or noted missing. He knew he should let well enough alone, but a curiosity tagged him as he and Doyle crossed the clearing toward the tunnel.

"That girl," he remarked, thumbing at the cabin, "where'd she come from? Netty and an old renegade like Brusilov. It's a funny setup."

"You don't know?" Doyle shrugged in surprise. "Fifteen, sixteen y'ar ago Netty was picked up by Quinnalt's band of Klickitat. She was too young to remember who she was, and only Quinnalt knows where he got her. He kept her with his own daughter for years. Brusilov seen her in the Klickitat camp and tried to buy her free. Quinnalt like to burst a blood pipe. Brusilov got the heave-ho, but he was on one of his loony spells, and thinkin' Netty was kin of his, stole her out of Quinnalt's lodge. Lord knows how. Been playin' hide-'n-seek ever since. At times Brusilov's aware she's jus' a strange white gal, and other times he believes she's blood, but sane or not, that defrocked Russ gave her good raisin'. Taught her everythin' he knew, then sent her to mission school at Yakima. Quinnalt found out and hit the place, but Brusilov got her out an hour ahead o' him and his braves. They discovered this hole then, an' hid here trappin', rarely poking their heads out . . ." Doyle paused, spotting Natasha seated cross-legged on the shadowy front stoop, and then he eyed Fargo suspiciously. "Say, you ain't gonna try messin' with her, are you?"

"Who, me?" Fargo said with wounded innocence, glimpsing the girl uncoil her legs and sashay their way. "Perish the thought."

"Good, 'cause Brusilov's vowed to perish the thoughtless," Doyle warned, then changed the subject as Netty approached. "Yep, Williard Hamilton allus had a streak of cat in him. But his own trappers, workin' on the starvation contracts he hands out, bucked him enough to keep his claws wore down to the quick. Why, g'morning, Netty. You're up early."

"Who can sleep?" she responded, falling in between them. "I agree, speaking of Hamilton. He was mostly talk and darn little action till this last winter. Something happened. He's turned strut-chested, on the prod."

"Can't figure it 'less someone's needling him or he's drinkin' a new brand o' courage oil. Wish we could be better help, Skye."

"The most help would be more men."

Doyle nodded. "Aye. Me'n Abel Bone was talkin'. They's some boys around Harts Pass on the upper Methow who didn't come in this spring. Like as not they been cut down by Yankee or Anglican wolves, but we reckoned it might be worth taking a gander for 'em. Still, even with 'em we're outgunned and outnumbered by them companies' posts. I sure hanker to hear you've talked Hamilton into pullin' in his horns when you return from Fort George."

Fargo grinned. "I'll give it my best shot."

"Whose horns?" Natasha asked, covertly sinking fingernails into Fargo's arms. "Are you going there hoping to give your shot to the owner of Anglican—or to his straw-haired daughter?"

Her question was razor-edged. Doyle blinked, perplexed, but Fargo felt its keenness and its steel, and he answered easily, "No man goes to a woman when there's fighting to be done."

Half an hour later, sweeping downriver, Skye Fargo thought about his reply. He had meant it honestly enough, yet he wondered if he hadn't been fudging a mite. Some years ago, when he'd first had dealings with Williard Hamilton, he'd been introduced to the Englishman's wife and their daughter, Celeste, who'd been about Natasha's age. On Fargo's infrequent visits since then, Hamilton remained aloof with that typical British reserve, especially after his wife died, while Celeste grew demandingly close, cool as ice and dangerous as fire. Now much depended on his mission to Fort George. If Hamilton had indeed changed for the worse, Celeste might prove influential. Fargo had no more idea what to expect of her than of her father, but he damn well would go to that woman if a deal could be struck. For if Hamilton chose to fight, the free trappers would be flanked by two deadly enemies, and more of their blood would be staining the white-water rivers.

Impatience rode Fargo. Against a wind-choppy current and thickening cloud veil, he held a grueling pace up the Columbia from the Nespelem to the junction at Kettle Falls, two days' voyage north and east of Zashcíta.

There, docking at the small Fort George pier, Fargo stepped ashore into a stockade that resembled an army garrison more than a trade post. A truculent, hostile tension was in the air, every man scowling curiously and heavily armed, even down to the Indian attendants. Two company trappers hurried into the main building as he started across the compound, while another gun-braced duo approached to cut him off, one of them touching his arm, halting him.

"I suppose you and your pard was bound in with a load o' fur. You got jumped, lost your fur, and your pard was killed. So you come in to square up."

Fargo eyed the pair. "Maybe."

"Maybe a damn free trapper, then!" The other Anglican fur man laughed, short and ugly. "Well, we got a welcome for you woods runners. Shuts a howl up faster'n anything you ever see. It goes like this!"

He and his companion bunched forward with anticipation. Fargo read their game, aware how two men could snag a troublemaker between them and swiftly deal him fierce punishment, intending no serious injury while rendering him harmless. As they closed, Fargo ducked down, straightening both arms out at once as he leapt upward again. He caught one full in the face, smashing him flat and kicking. The other man had turned away from that streaking blow, taking it on his shoulder. He roared, now, pawing at an enormous muzzle-loader in his belt.

Fargo jerked his own Colt free, saw the man was slow and deliberately stepped in. With a seemingly gentle wipe of the weapon, he laid its solid barrel against the man's head just under the edge of his cap. The blow made a sharp little sound like a tapped melon. The man dropped limply. Fargo turned and angled toward the main building, as around stood rooted Anglican fur men, surly and dark-countenanced, abruptly very careful under his scanning glance.

Before Fargo reached the building's front stoop, one of the trappers who'd rushed inside now hurried out the door marked OFFICE, followed by Celeste Hamilton. Five-seven, with the pink-and-white skin of the English, Celeste was no hothouse beauty. Her long blond hair was a bit frizzled, and her face was drawn by frontier hardship. Yet her face also showed character, her lips full, her hazel eyes alert, and her figure was lushly curvaceous. Celeste was gold and ivory where Natasha was jet and cream; a woman mature and contained, compared to a girl puckish and impulsive. They had only one point in common—they both belonged to the fur country. Well, two—they'd both besported with Fargo, a bond he hoped they'd never learn they shared.

There had been times when Celeste's self-possession had nettled him. Even now, despite the strain evident in her features, she still had her uppity manner.

"Skye Fargo," she greeted, as if stating a fact. "Why're you here?"

"Hello, Celeste. I've some business to discuss with your dad."

"I'm not sure how much discussing he'll do. Father was shot."

"*What?* How . . . when?"

"Sniper attack. A week ago, a rifleman climbed the tallest spruce there in the timber fringing the clearing. Sign indicates he stayed there several hours, till dusk, when Father came out of our quarters and

54

headed across to the warehouse. One shot was fired. It sheared Father's scalp, tore an ear off, came within a pip of killing him. The rifleman escaped. Our subfactor organized a search, but . . ." Celeste sighed, shaking her head.

Fargo glanced to the tree she indicated, its top visible above the palisade. It apparently stood well back in the timber from the edge of the clearing, a good half-mile from the compound. "One shot at dusk. At eight hundred yards. A fool's luck!"

"No! Not luck. Deliberate murder, by an expert marksman."

"Anglican?"

She stared at him scornfully. "Our men are all loyal and respect my father. You wish to know who it was? Tell him, Klute."

The trapper siding Celeste was Klute, a grizzle-bearded and buckskinned old regular that Fargo recalled from previous visits. He acknowledged Fargo with a nod, responding in a gravel voice, "They's three gents in all these parts could've made that shot. Only three. One of 'em is Malone, a hunter up in Pasayten wildwood. A Frenchy Canuck from Coeur d'Alene, name of La Croix, is another. The third is Leon Ives."

Celeste frowned irritably. "Leon is our subfactor," she snapped. "Why do you keep including him with those vicious riffraff?"

Klute shrugged. "Takes a sharpshootist to figure he'll hit target from as far as that tree. Ives got the skill an' knows it, so he could've done it."

"Utter nonsense," Celeste protested. "Come on, Skye, I'll bring you to Father."

Fargo trailed her as she returned to the building, admiring the sensuous motions of her hips, buttocks, and legs within the tight sheath of her taffeteen wrapper. Pushing open the office door, she ushered him into a small, square room already packed with eight scruffy, heavyset company trappers. With them stood a handsome, muscular fellow, with frank brown eyes, crisp chestnut hair, and mustache to match, garbed in a clean butternut shirt and frontier breeches. As he and Fargo silently appraised each other, Fargo knew instinctively that he must be Leon Ives; he was just the "propah soht" Hamilton would hire as subfactor.

At a battered curtain-top desk sat Williard Hamilton, wearing a gauze-bandage turban. He was as Fargo remembered him, a gaunt man with a high, intelligent forehead and gray Dundreary whiskers, stern of expression, calm and chill of manner. And yet now he also displayed an oddly intense stare and quick, twitchy movements that told Fargo Hamilton was not the same man he had last met.

Fargo ventured, "I'm sorry to hear you're hurt."

"Instead of dead?" Hamilton charged, his voice having an abrasive and peculiarly uneven tone. "There isn't any welcome for outsiders at Fort George, Skye Fargo. But you got past, so say your piece and get out."

Fargo, realizing Hamilton was deadly serious, replied equally brusquely. "Out on the Nespelem is a party of honest trappers who've turned pirate till they get back the furs stolen from them. They're just about to go after Red Jack Epinard's hide. If you don't want them here, call your dogs off the fur trails and open your post goods to free trade."

Hamilton made no immediate response, staring woodenly, seeming only barely able to understand the words. Instead, the man Fargo assumed was Leon Ives answered, chuckling coldly. "We'll be delighted to accept furs from your free trappers—as damages!"

"Damages," Fargo growled angrily. "What've they done to Anglican that they owe you or your boss damages?"

"What haven't they done, sir? Rather than work their own lines, all winter they've slipped over the ridges to rob company lines. Master Hamilton has seen with his own eyes, as we all have seen, the bodies of Anglican men taken from sprung traps, murdered, their catches stolen."

"Infernal free trappers!" Hamilton muttered, fixed-eyed, a malevolent smirk quirking his lips. "Enough of this flub-dub. It is clear that Fargo is one of 'em. Take him away, men, lock him up till we decide how to deal with these dastardly bush rats."

Celeste indignantly gasped, "Father!"

But Fargo didn't waste his breath on words. Trapped in the confining office, ringed by burly company men, he knew anything he might try to say would be laughed off. In desperation, he plunged for the door, slugging the nearest man in the solar plexus. Gagging, the trapper sagged, reeling and falling back against some of the others ganging up on Fargo.

Fargo launched himself at the next closest man, aware that he was in deep, perhaps fatal trouble if he failed to fight his way out of the office. Again he punched with his right fist, while his left struck at another man in a stiff-arm clout to the heart. The results were agonized gruntings and scuffled stumblings, yet even as Fargo pressed his attack, Leon Ives shoved in from behind, lashing with his re-volver. Seeing the looming rush, Fargo tried to duck and twist away, but he lacked sufficient space to elude the blow entirely. The gun barrel slashed at Fargo with stunning force, skewing his hat off, and something akin to a whole magazine of black powder exploded inside his head. He tried to keep his feet under him, but he felt himself sinking as the room darkened, and then he felt nothing more at all.

*　　*　　*

Gradually, reluctantly, Fargo recovered his senses. His body ached with pain, especially his rib cage, and his head pulsed with a dull ache as his wits slowly revived.

His mind had been blank after the subfactor whacked him unconscious, but it was evident that he'd been stripped of his weapons, then beaten and stomped some before being dumped on the dirty, straw-strewn floor of a dark tack room. It reeked of horse, and saddles and other gear were dimly visible in the moonlight angling through the room's grated window. Across from the window was a solid plank door, undoubtedly locked— At least, it didn't budge when Fargo lurched over and rammed against it. Carefully, then, he looked over the tack room for another way out or a weapon to use, but found nothing except the stub of a broken riding crop. A bitter dismay gripped him.

He was braced on stiff legs, gazing out through the bars of the window, when a sound behind him made him wheel. A key rasped in the outer lock, and on creaky hinges the door eased ajar. Celeste dipped inside, swinging the door closed with one hand while holding a towel and a bottle of liniment in the other.

"You fool!" Her eyes, though, contradicted her sharp mouth.

"Thanks for wising me up earlier," he replied dryly.

"Well, maybe that's why I got Klute to help me get you out now. But really, Skye, you should never have come here like you did today."

"I wouldn't have if I'd known that Fort George is a powder keg ruled by a man with scrambled brains."

"Father'll be all right. It's only that his nerves get too tight when he's under pressure." She paused, glaring at the cloth and bottle, then at Fargo. "Never mind him. Go sit or lie down somewhere, and take off your shirt."

"I'd prefer to go out the door and take off, period."

"So would I. It's not late enough, though, too many men still about. Some of them looted your canoe, and Klute's scrounging new supplies from our stores. He'll be here when he's done, but he must be cautious, bide his time. Now, stop arguing and let me clean you up a little. You took quite a beating."

Shrugging, Fargo went and stacked some smelly horse blankets on the floor, then removed his clothes above the waist and settled with his legs drawn up. Celeste, kneeling alongside, pulled the liniment bottle cork out with her teeth and began cleansing the open, blood-scabbed cut in his scalp. The liniment burned the way Thundermug whiskey burned his belly. Celeste, laughing as he flinched and sucked in his breath, swabbed his bruised face and midriff. "It's made to kill pests," she told him.

"If you want me dead, why're you trying to save me?"

"I can't stand to see any stray animal killed without a fighting chance. There, that's as good as I can do," she said, patting him dry. The wildness had gone out of her for the moment, and she trembled, vulnerable, pouting. "I think you're a danger, Skye Fargo."

He grinned at her, feeling stirrings, thinking *she* was the danger. His hand brushed her shoulder, his fingers combing a soft hanging mass of blond hair as he eyed her lips and breasts and legs, her dress hiked provocatively from the way she was sitting.

"Skye?"

"Yes."

"I want you alive. I want you now."

"You don't want me, Celeste. You're just upset."

"I am, but I also want you. This may be our last time. Quick, while we still have time." Swiftly she started to undress, unhooking her dress, then rising to slip it and her tie-string pantaloons off, everything including her ankle-high boots. "What're you waiting for? Lost your balls?"

For a moment Fargo did not move, could not move, his gaze feasting on her nudity. Her breasts were plump melons, nipples large and jutting like ripe cherries. Her belly, taut and flat, flared down into rich flaxen curls, the pink flesh of her vaginal lips peeking warmly from underneath. Her thighs were smooth and tapered into long legs that he knew would wrap around him in a squeezing grip of passion.

Then, goaded to recklessness, Fargo shucked his pants and boots, aroused, throbbingly erect, aching to penetrate her voluptuous body. Celeste laughed throatily as they sank back to the horse blankets, a woman in heat, and Fargo knew there was no longer any denying her . . . or himself.

His mouth closed on one of her nipples, sucking while he fondled her other breast. His other hand roamed down her body to the vee of her crotch, and moaning, she spread her legs slightly and moved her hips in concert with his rubbing hand. Soon she was so moist that he was able to ease three fingers up inside her, while her own hand slid between his legs in search of his swelling erection.

"My stallion," she sighed, stroking the shaft. "And I'm your old gray mare."

"Not old, not gray, and you're sure what you used to be."

Again Celeste laughed, low and liquid. Pushing him down, she straddled his pelvis with her knees on the blankets on either side of his hips. Gazing with eyes of passion, she rose and impaled herself on his fleshy spear, contracting her strong thighs so that the muscular action clamped her moistly welcome passage tightly around his member. Fargo gasped. She hovered above him, thrusting with her hip and buttock muscles, pumping on his hardening girth as fast as she could, pummeling Fargo against the floor.

His hands grasped her dancing breasts. "Not so hard!"

"Oh, your head, your poor head," she cooed, slowing. "I'm sorry. You just lie there and let me take you nice and easy."

Despite her best intentions, Celeste soon began humping wildly again, bouncing her hips up and down with increasing abandon. She pistoned her tightly gripping loins around his shaft until Fargo was no longer aware of his wound and was thrusting in rhythm to her frenzied tempo.

He sucked one swaying breast into his mouth, flicking her distended nipple with his tongue and grasping her other breast with his hand. She writhed and wriggled and squirmed in a dozen different directions. Fargo felt his excitement mounting higher and sensed he was on the brink of release. Her lustrous hair was a dizzying cloud in his eyes, the tang of her sweat was on his tongue, her dilated gaze glowed with ecstasy as, together, they hammered at yet a faster pace, pushing deeper, their sweating bodies slapping and rubbing tempestuously.

Celeste tried to say something, but she could no longer speak. She groaned, shuddering from the electric impact of her own orgasm, as the hot jets of Fargo's bursting climax flooded up into her belly. He pulled her tighter to his pulsing groin, as if he were trying to merge flesh and bone, then collapsed, Celeste falling across him, stretching her legs back so she could lie with him inside her.

After a long, languid moment, she murmured, "Better get up."

"Just was up."

"Up again, fast," she cried, jackknifing off Fargo's loins, as suddenly the sound of approaching bootsteps filtered through the door. Equally alarmed, Fargo sprang upright, hopped on one leg. "You're stepping on my pants!"

"Those're my bloomers," she retorted, frenziedly scurrying.

A moment later the door opened and Klute entered. "Hurry! Ives is comin', but there's yet a chance," he said, then noticed Fargo stuffing in a shirttail, and glancing back at Celeste, he saw that she didn't have her right boot on snugly. He grinned. "Well, I might've knowed."

"Why, you old goat, you've been trying to play slap 'n tickle with me all along," she retorted, darting out past Klute into the stable beyond.

Fargo was a pace behind her. Relocking the door, Klute caught up with them and they hastened along a short aisle of stalls to a side entrance. Outside, they plunged along the shadowed wall of the stable to the corner, where they paused to collect their breath and check the way ahead.

Klute pressed an aged Spiller & Burr percussion pistol into Fargo's hand. "Here. I was able to filch your rifle back, but Ives got your Colt and knife."

"Thanks. Celeste, you won't lose by this," Fargo promised softly. "I don't know who's robbed and killed Anglican men, but it's not the free trappers. They've suffered the same and are blaming the fur companies. It's a vicious circle, and I've a hunch someone's deliberately rigging it, trying to start up open war here. I'll do all I can to cool off the free trappers."

"Try," she begged. "Father's a proud man. In these woods, he's the last bastion of England south of Canada. He fought hard to build his company prestige here, and he'll fight just as hard to defend—"

She fell silent. They flattened themselves against the wall, statues not daring to breathe as they heard Leon Ives and another man nearing the stable.

"True, when Old Man Hamilton dies, Miss Celeste becomes owner," Ives was saying to his companion. "But I'd be boss. She'd have no choice."

"Not if she wanted any of the men to stay signed on," the other agreed as they entered the stable through the front double doors. "We dance with a woman. We eat her cooking, and maybe so sing to her. But we won't work for one, by thunder!"

Fargo glanced at Celeste, who was flushed. He stepped forward, then, finger to his lips before she or Klute could utter a protest, and sprinted on cat feet around the corner to the front doorway. Sliding inside, pressed against the inner wall, he listened hard as he scanned the murky interior, then worked his way closer to the men. He had to get them swiftly and silently, before they saw him coming or discovered he'd escaped, before any shot or alarm rousted others in the fort. They stopped in front of the tack-room door, Ives fumbling for the key while his companion patted his pockets.

"You got any makin's, Leon? I crave a smoke."

"Jesus. At a time like this?"

"Hey, even a condemned man gets a last puff, y'know."

"You're just jumpy. Nothing to be scared of, helping our prisoner to suicide with his own gun." Ives laughed and the man cursed, so close to Fargo that he could hear the rustle of papers as they rolled cigarettes. There was a flare of a match, and he glimpsed them huddling to get lights. He launched forward then, hurtling from the darkness to crash into them, his full weight colliding with their hunched shoulders. While they staggered and fought for balance, he gun-whipped and punched with brutal swiftness, clubbing the neck of the second man. That one crumpled, groaning. Fargo felt arms go around him from behind. He put all his strength into his back and lifted, flinging Ives sidewise, slamming him into the door, then pivoting to clout him unconscious.

Quickly Fargo removed his weapons and the door key from the subfactor's comatose body. Unlocking the tack room, he dragged both men inside, tore the liniment towel into strips for gags, and bound them hand and foot with bridle straps. Then taking the liniment bottle, which Celeste had forgotten in her haste, Fargo relocked the door and rushed back outside.

"Well?" she asked, almost fearfully.

"Well, now my escape will be blamed on Ives instead of you," Fargo replied, handing her the incriminating bottle.

"Damn his black soul," Klute growled as Fargo returned the old percussion pistol with thanks. "Williard Hamilton was runnin' about the squarest company post you'd ever see till he hired Ives for subfactor."

Celeste snapped, "I thought I made myself clear, Klute. I don't wish to hear any more such twaddle, and this certainly isn't the time nor the place."

Klute nodded, muttering. They raced hunching across an open area and dived in behind a tool shanty, then skirted around to a narrow lane that ran like an inky sewer alongside the sharpened log stockade.

Obstinately, Klute refused to keep silent, and as they went, he whispered in panting wheezes, "Everybody was doin' comfortable. But Ives no more got here and settled in when more recruits started followin' him in. More recruits than we had streams to work. Ives talked Hamilton into takin' 'em on. And right the same time, some of our boys started gettin' bushwhacked. Independents, owl-hootin', Ives said, and it looked almighty like it. Only them that got ambushed wasn't ever the new lads. Just old duffers like me, gents that swore by Hamilton and didn't give a Paiute damn for Ives. Now Hamilton's off his toes an' Ives is noisin' about takin' over the post. What's worse, he'll hafta take Miss Celeste to do it."

Fargo gripped Celeste by the arm. "He's right. It isn't safe for you here, Celeste. Come with me."

She shook her head. "No, Skye. Something's come over Father, and I've got to find out what's squeezing down on him and end it. In any case I'm a Hamilton. I'll stick by Anglican, whatever Father does, whatever happens."

Klute was shaking his head glumly to this as they came to a small, heavily barred door at the lower end of the enclosure. Tugging on the crossbars, he complained to Fargo, "I've knowed stubborn gents in my day, but nary a one could shake salt onto this gal. Her pa trusted Leon Ives, so she'll trust him till hell freezes—or it's too late."

With the crossbars back, they sneaked through. Celeste caught Fargo's sleeve outside the stockade and pointed to the dark river. "Your canoe's loaded and ready to go."

"You mean—"

"I mean shove off, outlander, and stay long gone from Fort George!" Celeste strode away, heading briskly for the lamplit main building.

6

Moments later, Skye Fargo was on the water.

He covered forty miles without a stop, and while plying the turbulent current of the Columbia, he pondered the puzzling situation.

It was pretty plain from the attack on the rendezvous that Red Jack Epinard was at least partly responsible for the bloodshed. Not at all clear was why or who lay behind his action. And Williard Hamilton presented still more of a puzzle. The Anglican fur owner was a smart boss—in health at least. It was hard to believe he would order a campaign against the free trappers, especially not if Celeste had anything to say about it. And it did appear as if the Anglican men had been victims of the same sort of sneaky attacks that had been thinning the ranks of Modoc Doyle's old friends. Was the Yankee company out to rid the territory of all competition by playing the free trappers off against the Anglican men? It seemed too obvious a ploy.

Fargo took a rest break, then plunged on through the night. Shortly after another cloud-obscured dawn, he glimpsed an Indian fishing from a partially submerged rock. The startled Klickitat dropped his line and fish and was left quickly behind as Fargo swept downstream. But the Trailsman was well aware that word would speed ahead of him as if on the wind, and there could well be other meetings not quite so accidental.

At nightfall, bitterly weary from bending his paddle for endless hours, Fargo came to the confluence of the Sanpoil and the Columbia and beached his canoe in some thick brush. All day he had been on edge, anticipating a confrontation with the Klickitat. Their sign in the area was plentiful, and he'd been forced to haul himself out of the river three times to hide from small parties of Indians that had passed him from behind. Adding annoyance, the long-threatened storm front had slowly begun to roll through from the northeast. Earlier it had sprinkled off and on, and as the light waned, so had the temperature, till Fargo could feel a slight yet distinct bite in the air, a chill that presaged the cold night to come.

Now, still thirty miles from Zashcíta and too exhausted to drive on, Fargo would have liked a fire and a hot meal. But he made it a dry camp, rolling into his sugan in the brush beside his canoe. An hour later, he snapped awake to hear a strange sound trilling up the river, a *chanson* sung by a solitary feminine voice:

> Some die young,
> Others die old.
> Runners of the woods,
> Hunters of the fur,
> Live forev-ver . . . !

The voice moved closer, the singer apparently skirting the near bank with her canoe. Fargo tumbled from his bedroll with a curse. Natasha! Rowing upriver into all this Indian sign, her voice caroling out ahead of her, and her brains obviously left far behind.

Fargo was up to his thighs in the water when Natasha came abreast in the darkness. Afraid to raise a shout loud enough to break through her soprano chant, he smacked the palm of his hand down flat onto the water with a smart chop. The sound was like that of a beaver's tail, warning a colony of coming danger. Natasha choked off in midsyllable and, leaning against her paddle, spun her dugout in toward the brush. Fargo caught its blunt prow and towed it on in, and as it hit the bank, Natasha piled over its side, squinting.

"Skye! I was—"

"Quiet!" Fargo began trotting back to his canoe.

Sprinting after, Natasha snapped, "Why? What is it?"

"Klickitat." As he buckled on his shell belt, he spied a slight movement in the surrounding foliage and glimpsed a dark head uplifted with an eagle feather wavering in the cool night breeze. Snatching up his Sharps, he called softly over his shoulder, "We've got to hit higher ground before we're cut off. C'mon!"

Natasha didn't question further, those last clipped words having answered everything she needed to know. Her hand went into his and they were running, dodging between boulders and bushes, across open patches, and into the deep hillside timber beyond. But the Indians were ahead of them. In the first three hundred feet they flung themselves prone twice just in time to avoid streaking braves.

The third time they were not so lucky. No single warrior, but a wide-flung, hawkeyed net swept toward them. Shadowy forms charged from the underbrush, and they were surrounded by painted Klickitat braves, leveling lances tipped with blades secured from Russian traders years before.

Fargo felt a chill shimmy along his spine as he

stopped short, holding his rifle high above his head with both hands. Grunting satisfaction, the Indians took his weapons and tightened a noose of braided horsehair around his neck. Natasha put up a short, quick struggle, biting and kicking while flailing with her fists when they attempted to lasso her. She caused little damage and much amusement. Then they were led north at a fast trot through heavy timber and rugged foothills on the eastern side of the Sanpoil.

For ceaseless hours they were yanked onward, given no chance to speak or to rest, callously dragged if they stumbled or balked. Eventually the party lurched downslope to the river, where another nameless mountain tributary was disgorging torrents into an already deep cascade. Here the swift-flowing channels met at a sharp angle, converging along two sides of a narrow gravel spit and pooling in a riptide of currents. Near the bank, began willow saplings and common variety of grasses, briar, and shrubby vegetation. In this straggly fringe was an Indian encampment. Some cook fires were burning, but there were no lodges, indicating it was merely a layover spot for one of the several hunting parties whose sign had troubled Fargo that day.

Fargo and Natasha were reined to a halt by the largest fire. The braves huddled to chew things over, and as those already in camp joined in their opinions, an impromptu camp council developed. Fargo, listening, recognized their lingo as rooted in Shahaptian, the region's predominant Indian tongue, but spoken too fast and thick in an unfamiliar tribal dialect for him to follow clearly. He glanced at Natasha, standing ashen-faced yet resolute, aware as he that they mustn't display fear.

He whispered, "What's the talk about?"

"The usual. When and how to slay us." Abruptly, anxiously she eyed him. "Skye, don't tell me you can't speak a word. If they come to jaw, I can't do the talking. Not a woman's place. Besides, I couldn't help sounding like a native, and that'd give me away for sure."

"Surprising nobody has recognized or at least suspected you yet," Fargo murmured as he recalled Doyle's story of Brusilov rescuing Natasha and Chief Quinnalt's efforts to recapture her. "Relax, I reckon I can hold a simple palaver. But if it comes down to final parting words, you say them and save yourself."

"Balls," she hissed. "It's a young group with the marks of outlying clans. They don't remember me from before, back when they were cubs far from the main camp, so why care about me now—except as an excuse to run renegade. Catching and bringing me in ends their fun. You want to bet how fast they kill us both, to make sure I'm not found again?"

Fargo nodded, acknowledging but not entirely convinced by her argument. There was no time to pursue it, for the powwow was breaking up, the Indians coming to gather around, glowering and gesturing. From the cluster emerged a stocky, ferociously scarred brave whose buckskins were heavily worked with beads and quills, the long fringes affixed to many tiny trade bells that tinkled as he approached. Apparently the camp leader, he stared at his prisoners for a long time in haughty silence. They stared back, defiant.

Finally the brave demanded, "Where would the paleskin go? What do you take of our land?" He was asking Fargo but kept studying Natasha.

"I go as I will," Fargo countered with equal disdain. "And I require the welcome your unfriendly camp denies us, the comfort of your robes and food for my squaw to prepare. Hurry! Do not keep us waiting."

The brave wasn't checking Natasha now; Fargo had hooked his attention, all right, and his eyes glittered menacingly. "You chatter," he replied, "like a magpie flapping above heads of the great four-footed hunters. Your noise is merely annoying."

Not much as insults went, Fargo thought, but it made a hit with the local audience. A rousing "How, how, how!" was chanted to the thump of lances. When the sidelines quieted, the brave got down to business, his scarred face looking both arrogant and deadpan.

"Hear our answer. For many years you paleskins have roved among us, and there has been room. Now that paleskins make war among themselves, now there is no longer room. Now Chief Quinnalt has need of Tahtzi, the pale girl who was his daughter. I think I will take him your squaw."

Fargo shrugged nonchalantly.

"Ah, you don't mind. She is not your squaw, I think. She is what you try to take from our land, the missing child Tahtzi." The brave again scrutinized Natasha, who maintained her act as a scrappy victim of mistaken identity. "Mmm . . . What name do you call her?"

"Dolores," Fargo stated, the first name that occurred to him. "The same name her folks back in Ohio always claimed she's christened. You got her mixed up with someone else, for a fact."

"Our chief will set her free then, no harm done. No harm a squaw minds," the brave added slyly. "But accidents may happen. Often."

Fargo scented bait—the dangling insinuation of rape by hordes of Indians. Doubtful. As a rule, Indians considered white women more bad-smelling than sexually appealing. This was a trick to lure a rise out of him; a man goaded to an anguished dither will act on emotion, impulsively blabbing all, giving all, to gain his driven goal.

"You harm yourself, not her. Or do you prefer poverty to money and power?" Fargo scathed. "Do-

71

lores has provided me well for five years now, and I figure my care can pull two, three more good seasons from her. Seems blind foolish to waste her, so how about a partnership? Worth a private talk, at least, away from wind and ears."

The brave gaped, taken aback for a moment. Then he moved toward Natasha, as if to test Fargo's sincerity by copping a feel of the merchandise. Natasha cast a stony warning glare, standing her ground. Grinning, the brave closed and abruptly struck, his open-palmed hands glomming over her breasts.

Natasha blew berserk, cycloning kicks, jabs, and bites at the brave, who beat a hasty retreat, to the hooting guffaws of the bystanders, while Fargo angled in toward Natasha. She was straining on her rope leash like a rabid dog, snapping and clawing at the buck.

"You scummy suck-egg lizard," she raged, blessedly in English. "I'll roast your stinkin' liver on a stick, you—"

She was cut short by a clack of her teeth as Fargo brought up his right fist and hit her square on the chin. Natasha arched back, windmilling, and landed on her fanny, sitting upright with her legs outstretched. She looked at Fargo with a dazed, querulous perplexity, one hand rubbing her jaw.

The brave was impressed. He also was livid, smarting from loss of face. He stood awhile in stewing thought, then told Fargo, "Piss on your offer, now I make you mine. You say where Tahtzi is. If true, you leave alive. Otherwise . . ."

"Hell! How should I know where she is?"

"Tahtzi was stolen by a paleskin. You are a paleskin, so you know where to find her. Tell us where else, if not here playing your squaw."

"One squaw keeps me too busy to look out for others, but I'd sure know if anyone was posing as her," he retorted, and broke out laughing with gusto, becoming savage then, stabbing a finger at the brave. "I hold my woman. You lost Tahtzi. If she was swiped, it was under your noses, in your own land. You lost her and she's long gone, while you prowl around like coyotes rooting campfire ashes."

The brave stiffened, the muscles of his cheeks and neck pulsating, a malevolent spark to his eye. "Enough for tonight now. I am tired, hungry, and we must prepare the deer. The night is chilling, too. A man thinks best when cold, so best we stake you outside, yes. I dislike paleskins, above all skinners, and crave to see you dead. But your lives I will trade you for information. That is my bargain for a few hours more."

Given a word and wave of command, a half-dozen braves pounced on their captives, bound them securely hand and foot, and dragged them out to the end of the gravel spit. When the Indians had moved away, Natasha swore heartily, cussing Fargo while she was at it.

"I've never been so eager to hit a man! Peddling me as a slut was vile, but damn you, knocking me down like one was going too far."

"Tough. A sock on the chin beats a slip of the tongue, and the way you were raving, you'd have spouted Klickitat or Russian before you knew what you were doing. We've gained some extra time, but that smart devil has called our bluff."

"Let him call. He won't hear different," Natasha vowed.

"Sure," Fargo agreed grimly. "But we'll be a mite uncomfortable while he's trying. You know firsthand better than I do, I reckon, how they go about prying out what they want with hot sticks. Me, I only met one man that could walk after a digging like that. And he was blind as a bat."

Natasha fell morosely silent. Fargo watched the

camp before him prepare their meal, the deer carcass from some previous hunt sizzling over the flames. His own famished belly gurgled as the air swirled with the redolence of burning pine wood and the aroma of cooking venison. And with it the chill breeze rose to sharp, nippy gusts that cut through good buckskin like steel.

He flexed his numbing limbs, pumping circulation while testing the rope. It was tight and well-knotted, but not quite tight enough or knotted enough, he sensed. Natasha was quick to catch on and began checking her bonds, and for a long while they labored to weaken points that might, given time and effort, just loosen enough for them to slip free. They worked covertly, avoiding suspicion, appearing trussed immobile when three braves and the leader strutted over.

"Comfortable?" the leader taunted. "No need to wait to talk with me. I have good fire, plenty warm robes. A wise man could sleep by the fire—"

"I'll see enough fire when I'm dead," Fargo snarled as Natasha bared her teeth. "Get the hell away from here and leave us to rot."

The leader shrugged and turned chuckling back toward the camp. The other braves fell in beside him, talking rapidly.

"Blast his pemmicaned hide," Natasha fumed. "Did you notice he hasn't sent a runner for the chief or anyone to identify me? He doesn't care who I am. He just plans to have a little fun."

"Figures. He'd be crossing his chief, though; everyone would. And what's this lie about Quinnalt needing his kid? I couldn't fit the connection between paleskins and war and room in the land and her, er, you."

"No lie. That's the chief's excuse for trouble, his style of guff. I don't know what he's up to, either, except up to no good. Probably he's got an oily scheme in his pouch that he wants me for, or he wouldn't be looking so hard. But I'm pretty certain something else is up, too. Quinnalt's a wily old devil and he'll do what it takes to get his way and worry about the cost later. If he was to join Red Jack Epinard, we'd have a plenty tough steak to chew."

"Is that why you went sailing by yourself, to find out?"

"Of course. I often go alone," she replied blithely. "I learned these hills a long time ago. I'm safer moving in them at will, than burrowing in at home to be cornered." She nuzzled his chest, cuddling for warmth, and with a yawn, added, " 'Sides, I missed you."

Fargo said no more about the foolishness of the trip. Any advice would've hit deaf ears, particularly now, for despite her being bound and curved awkwardly against him, Natasha had promptly dropped into an exhausted sleep.

Shifting her so he could maneuver, Fargo continued to strain and twist on the rope. He scanned the surrounding dark spit, but glimpsed nothing that might help; even the stones were smoothed of sharp edges by water's flow. The converging channels of the Sanpoil River and its branch were roiling cascades, swollen from melted snows up at their headwater summits, rock-ripping and dappling white spray as they merged and thundered on south.

On all sides the black landscape was peaceful, and at the camp, braves were conversing low and desultory after their heavy venison feed. Natasha nestled, breathing in profound slumber. But Fargo's mind was too busy for sleep as he turned his focus to the camp. The light was low and so was he, but he tried working out potential routes through the gloom ahead while continuing to pressure his bound wrists and legs. He was still at it an hour later when the braves were all bunched around the embers of their fires, snoring. And he kept on, worrying the rope while searching to find an overlooked way. Two paths were already in mind: one went to the scar-faced leader; the other to the humongous, liver-lipped son of a bitch who'd taken Fargo's weapons—but there seemed no way out of the main camp. As far as Fargo could judge, a cat couldn't have crept past the camp and through the woodsy fringe without rousing someone.

7

"Time to go," Fargo said, awakening Natasha.

"Won'ful," Natasha murmured. "How, by wings?"

"Water."

"The river?" Startled, she drew alert. "Lucifer! I'd rather crawl through fire than jump in that current in this weather."

"We're not hemmed in by fire," Fargo replied tersely, and set to maneuvering them around, playing slack he'd drawn from the tether. With Natasha helping, they arranged to be more or less facing each other, Fargo then indicating his tied wrists. "The knot slips a little. Try to pull it."

It proved difficult; Natasha's own hands were so tightly looped that she couldn't manipulate her fingers very easily. Frustrated, she bent forward and caught a stubborn loop in her teeth, tugging while plucking with her fingers. Tenacious, she continued wrenching on the knot until eventually an end unraveled and the rope fell off Fargo's wrists.

"Good," he sighed. "Now you."

He set to work. It didn't take long for him to conclude he'd have to use his teeth to draw the knots. Leaning, he bit hold of the acrid-tasting strands of rope, his head brushing against her breasts as he

yanked, his hands plying, again, again . . . until
Natasha moaned softly.

"What's wrong, Netty? Did I hurt you?"

"Far from it, Skye. Keep working, I feel things
coming apart."

Fargo slaved on. At last the bonds dropped free,
and Natasha stretched her aching arms to revive
circulation while he untied their legs. For a moment
he looked over the old, worn ropes, which were
fashioned from scrap lengths of older, more worn
ropes knotted together; picking a piece up, he stood
and promptly lurched, suddenly gimpy on his muscle-
cramped legs. "Netty, can you walk?"

"If I can't, I'll crawl."

"Well, move about some, then strip."

"Naked?"

"Buff starkers. We've got to keep dry clothes to
put on when we land, or we'll never have a chance."

Natasha moaned. "A bullet's quicker—and more
pleasant." But she began to undress while Fargo
peeled deftly out of his gear. After the jacket, she
gathered the folds of her large shirt and hoisted it
over her head, tugging with crossed arms to pull the
bunched clothes past the bulge of her breasts. Bared
to the biting wind, the tips jutted upward and the
flesh was firm and high.

With her boots off, Natasha looked more vulnerable
than ever. Fargo, now also bare, grinned encourag-
ingly at her as he gathered his clothes. Timidly, but
resolutely, Natasha unbuttoned her pants, and as
they fell, she pulled her bloomers off with three
quick gestures: first she slid her palms along her
sides under the tie-top waistband; she pushed the
clinging material down her thighs and ankles; then
she kicked with her pants. She didn't try to hide the
velvety black accent mark at her crotch, although
her hands fluttered a little, as if she wanted to but
was determined not to. Her face was flushed, but

mingled with the expression of shame was a glimmer of triumph. She seemed to be boasting. "There! I did it!"

Instead she pleaded, "Let's get going before anyone wakes up."

"Soon's we make a float." Fargo straightened from a half-crouch, his skin already stung to a fiery tingle by the wind, and handed Natasha some short lengths of driftwood he'd scavenged as she'd finished disrobing. "Here, lash them together with the ropes. Tie the clothes on. Wrap them in my coat first, to help keep them dry getting across. I should be back by then, but if not, start hauling it to the water. If I'm not back by then, or it's plain I won't be getting back, shove off."

"But—"

"Get bustling. If I come hotfooting back, your doing is done." Fargo loped swiftly toward the camp, keeping low and watching he wasn't spotted. By following his carefully plotted mental trail, he avoided loose rock and other noisy pitfalls, his bare feet padding silently across the open stretch. He maintained this headlong sprint until he reached the comparative safety of a shrub clump some ten yards out from the general cluster of the camp.

There he crouched, studying the braves, listening to sleep sounds for other stirrings. He checked out his route, varying it slightly, then began to sneak carefully toward the scar-faced leader. He clung to what shadow and growth he could find, and about midway there, feeling as exposed as a newborn babe, he opined that perhaps he should have stripped after he got back. After all, he was slinking through a camp of warriors sworn to kill him, stark staring naked except for that length of rope he'd picked up, which was looped around his waist and slip-knotted like a trouserless belt. On the other hand, if he had to run for it, this way his clothes were packed, the float was done, and Natasha was ready. Besides, clothes wouldn't give him one whit of protection. Gliding on, Fargo decided he probably was better off with his clothes off.

Breathlessly he treaded his advance, gauging each footfall as though he were treading on eggs. When at last he reached the boulder nearest the dozing leader, he drew against it and removed his rope belt. Basically similar to the other ropes, it chanced to be the three-foot or so length he wanted, was a bit thinner, and braided of maguey—hinting it was a remnant of cow-busting lariat, younger than the horsehair pieces.

Flexing the rope, Fargo stood listening while he scanned the camp. Discounting the discord of concerted snoring, all was quiet. By luck, both braves he wanted to visit were along the near side, toward the fringe of the camp, where sleepers were more spaced out. His left hand holding the rope in the middle, he tiptoed to the leader, who was stretched mostly on his belly in an disarray of robes. A swift glance about, a final silent tread . . .

Fargo struck. Landing with his knee in the leader's back, he swung his left hand from the right shoulder to the right side of the leader's neck. The leader raised his head, the predictable reaction, and Fargo caught the flying end of his rope with his right hand on the left side of the leader's neck. The effect was a split-second rear cross choke. Simultaneously bearing down his knee in the small of the back, Fargo jerked the head and shoulders backward, breaking the spinal column. The leader died without a sound.

Quickly Fargo retied his rope belt and rummaged through the dead brave's meager personals. He took a single-edged butcher blade of a hunting knife, and after tucking the body back into bed, he wrapped himself in the largest robe and moved on.

This next path was a mite trickier, for it threaded by a number of sleepers. In a sense Fargo was sorry that it had to be this guy, because if it had been anybody else in the camp, he'd only have had to kill once instead of twice. His rope trick strangled normal folks splendidly, but the neck on that monstrous brave was the girth of a bison's thigh. Fargo had serious doubts he could choke him at all, but certainly not rapidly enough to avoid annihilation. So he'd had to throttle someone else to get a weapon to retrieve his weapons. The leader was simply the leading candidate. Fargo was brokenhearted over that, but he damn well hated the extra time and movement the killing took.

Swaddled to the eyeballs, assuming a flat-footed shuffle, Fargo approached with extreme caution. He carefully gauged each location, deciding his next stop and then taking advantage of anything possible in between to trundle there undetected. Finally he could feel his way to the black shelter of brush in which the Klickitat giant was bedded. He snaked in closer, parting limbs and twigs, the leader's knife clasped ready . . .

A low, gruff challenge came from the shadows. A moose rose out of the undergrowth, a human moose lunging at Fargo. Too late he saw the flash of the white man's knife. His mouth opened, but his yell of warning died aborn in the rattling croak as the Trailsman ripped wide his throat. The enormous brave toppled as a great tree might, cracking and snapping and earth-shaking landing, while Fargo darted to the bedroll, scattering it apart. Out rolled the Sharps. The holstered revolver took a few seconds longer, fanning the fire storm in his nerves. The brave was still thrashing, relatively feebly but very loud to Fargo, who wondered if the brave was dying, or was already dead and parts of him just hadn't heard the news yet. In any case, faint as the sounds may have been, they had been enough to spread warning. The camp was starting to stir.

Fargo ran. He shed the encumbering robe, hoisted his weapons, and ran full out, refusing to slow and thus risking a misstep as he skimmed the rough ground. Whiplike branches slashed at him at first, followed by thorny vines scratching his skin. That gave way to the exposed open flat of the spit. His ankle turned under him from rolling gravel, but on he sped, while sweat poured down his face and a howling frenzy was building behind him.

"Hit fast," he yelled at Natasha, angling toward her. She had the float almost to the water, but paused in her efforts when she saw him approaching with his guns. Panting breathlessly, Fargo hastily wedged them into the bundled clothes, flashing Natasha a grin. "Come on now, hit the water and don't quit fighting till you've got the sand of the other bank under your toes."

Seizing the little raft, Fargo sprinted to the bank, Natasha a pace behind. Arching out, they sliced feetfirst into the water as cleanly and silently as a thrown knife. The current seized their bodies and rushed their feet out from under them even before they could feel the terrible, viselike clamp of the mountain water.

Holding aloft the bundle of clothes, which barely splashed the surface when he hit the water, Fargo stroked clumsily with his free hand. Every muscle in his lower body doubled into a cramped, frantically protesting knot. A dead numbness started in his legs and rushed upward with breath-crushing swiftness, and defenseless, he was caught by the fast-scudding tide. Peripherally he glimpsed waving arms, then saw Natasha sweeping with him in the current, bobbing up and down in the foam, the sound of water roaring in their ears.

Abruptly, unexpectedly, the flow lifted him high

over some hidden object and hurled him against a massive jumble of rocks. He clung onto the float, hoisting it over his head, while his other hand clawed for a handhold. There was nothing there to grasp, just rock made glassy by the spray. He felt himself sliding away.

Then a towering swell burst over him and Natasha, its breaking wave submerging his head. A terrible temptation existed for a blinding instant to fill his lungs and stay under. He fought back to the surface, fearing he might have doused the clothes. But Natasha's well-built raft had saved them. Half-drowned, they wrestled loose of the tugging current and struck for shore, hardly able to keep from being dashed into a morass of jagged boulders through which the river was boiling in deadly rapids.

His toes touched sand, but he couldn't make them grip and the contact was lost. He slammed into a rock with savage force, then twisted away. The far bank seemed distant miles away. Again he shoved the float high into the air. Close at hand he saw the wake of Natasha's trim body. Then something closer whipped painfully across his face. He reached upward in a reflex to fend the lash away, and he caught the dripping tendrils of a willow branch. His fingers locked. Pulling strongly, he forced his numbed arms to snake around it. Once he had gripped the log securely, he started crawling, inch by inch, up its slanted trunk into a break in the bank. Ahead he saw shallows; behind he saw Natasha floundering weakly.

When his bone-cold feet scraped against stone, he dug in his toes for leverage and half-climbed, half-crawled to the end of the break. Here the ground lifted in a low hump, and he tossed the float up onto the bank. Then he returned to help Natasha, lifting her head from the water by her hair while, again one-handed, he swam, guiding her once more for the bank. Tossing her up after the clothes was impossible, and the slope of the bank was mossy slick. Only by snatching grass tufts and twiggy scrub was Fargo able to haul them both out.

Panting, slumping for a moment, Fargo realized that Natasha remained as he'd placed her, on her back, her eyes closed, arms wide. Alarmed, his initial impulse was to press an ear to her chest. But then he saw the rhythmic motion of her breasts, the lift of her sleek abdomen, the pulse of her parted thighs like the nervosity of a timid animal.

"You're breathing," he said. "Get up."

"Of course I'm breathing," she whispered hoarsely. "It's all I can handle right now."

"Dammit, get up! We'll be ass-deep in braves any second."

"Caught buck-naked, eh?" she quipped as Fargo hurried to the driftwood raft. Hunkering, back turned while he tore at the knots, he heard her sitting up, coughing, spitting a little water. Ropes loosened, he was hastening to open the freed bundle when Natasha let fly an ear-piercing screech.

Fargo pivoted, glimpsing the virulent features and ragged buckskins of one of the renegade Klickitats. The brave was wrestling to pin Natasha, stabbing at her with a trade hunting knife. Natasha, twisting onto her back as she went under him, managed to grab his knife wrist and hold it away from her chest, her other hand clawing his face, scratching for his eyes. Their struggle was frenzied and enmeshed, yet her fury was no match for his brawn, and the Indian bore down to impale her.

Searching frantically, Fargo saw the tip of the blade beginning to pierce her left breast just as his hand touched the butt of his revolver. There was no time to check its condition or take careful aim. He didn't try. He ripped the Colt out from the bundle and snap-triggered as he swung level.

The revolver fired in a satisfying blast of gun flame and powder. The hastily fired bullet struck the brave between the nape of his neck and his ear, rupturing his brainpan and blowing his skull apart. Like a spent lover, he collapsed limply across Natasha.

Fargo sprang to help Natasha as she thrashed out from beneath the body. Hysterical, her left breast flicked by a thin gash, she clung to him. Breaking her embrace, he grasped her by the hand and rushed her over to the mussed-apart bundle, speaking in a clipped, urgent voice.

"No time. Our uproar will bring them like flies to shi, eh, sugar. No time to dress, even. We'll have to take our stuff along. Quick!"

Feverishly they repacked and tied the bundle tight. Rigging a rope strap, Fargo swung the bundle across his back, grabbed his revolver, and with Natasha set off at a trot. It was hard going, to plunge on immediately like this. But there could be no waiting, no stopping, for two reasons.

They had fled the spit with the camp aroused, unfortunately, so now the braves were all out stalking in force. They had washed ashore on the same side as the Indians. Trying to cross the river again was out; they had no float and would surely be spotted. They had to stay on this side, moving ahead of the vindictive renegades.

The other reason was exposure. They were healthy; maybe they'd be fine. But this kind of chill weather, cold water, and shock together caused more deaths in spring or autumn than freezing blizzards ever did in winter. Naked, their only hope of warming their blood and restoring normal circulation was brisk, unrelenting exercise.

Angling inland, they climbed brush-clad banks and dipped along stony gulches, sloping higher through woods. The darkness around and especially toward the river was alive with soft movements of vegetation and occasional snaps of dry limbs. Fargo didn't need to see faces and bodies to know they had left none too soon.

Natasha guided them on a wide, looping detour to avoid some rough patches while veering more downriver. Rugged rocks and spurs loomed closer ahead; searching diligently, Fargo spied the dark mouth of a narrow canyon. It was off their course and might prove to be a box, trapping them. Yet its stone walls loomed high, offering shelter that the river basin and the rolling valley behind it could not. Stopping, he explained his notion. Then they both shut up, glancing back the way they had come. The noises of men were louder, indicating their trail was being followed, although damned if Fargo could figure out how. He had no intention of sticking around to ask, either.

As quietly as possible, they raced up and into the canyon. It made a turn, then another, and the slopes grew steeper. They saw a slim gully off to one side and darted into its narrow mouth, then twisted up into the rocks. Knowing it would be rank folly to try hiding at this point, they continued climbing the steep grade.

Fargo began wondering if perhaps he was suffering a mite of overexposure, or if the river swim had sapped too much out of him. The air he sucked into his lungs was becoming a two-edged sword, seeming to slice through tissue coming and going. In moments he was panting beside Natasha. She glanced at him and went on toward the top, motioning him to follow. Uninhibited, she had a fluid grace of movement, an effortless ease that defied him. When he reached the crest, he was gasping hard.

Natasha laughed. "A mountain man? Ha! More like a swamp bear." The imps in her eyes danced as she paced a few steps onward, only to grow startled as, with a muffled cry, she tripped and fell over the rim.

Fargo plunged after, dropping down the far side's grade of loose rock. They continued descending at a break-leg gait, Fargo feeling an easing in his chest. A cadence began to lift his stride and steady it, and his harsh breathing dropped to a quieter, less alarming tempo.

Shortly, as they wound lower along the jagged slopes, the brush grew heavy with briars and thorny weeds. The sound of voices came to them from their right, toward the valley, and they dived into the briar thickets as their hunters trampled nearer. Pressing on through the stinging thorns and nettles was torment supreme, like an insidious torture that won't kill its victim, only make him wish it would. Eyes watering, Natasha was biting hard on her knuckles to keep from crying out, while prancing with lively grace to avoid stepping on the ground cover of nettles. Watching her almost distracted Fargo from the pain he was suffering, feeling a growing admiration for her tenacity, her ardor, her spirit, her nubile breasts swaying. Most seductive, he thought.

They came to a steep gully then and slid down among the boulders along the shadowy floor. Above and behind them, men were beating around the briars. The turmoil masked Fargo's and Natasha's crawl up the opposite bank. Fargo forged ahead through the switching weeds, Natasha a wisp of pearlescence ahead of him in the darkness. They came to a small dusty clearing, the hardpan too solid to sustain even the meagerest of thistles.

"Let's take a rest," Natasha whispered. "We'll hear them if they come." She slumped to the ground, Fargo sagging alongside her, lungs straining for air, listening to their pursuers fade in the wrong direction.

"I think we shook them," Fargo panted. "For a while."

"Not long enough for us to get to our boats."

"That'll be a problem the whole way." Fargo sat up, removing the bundle from across his back. "The immediate problem is that the braves have moved betweeen us and the way to our boats, that's the problem."

Natasha stared at him, smiling wryly, then snuggled closer. "So we must burrow for a while, I suppose," she murmured, and a shiver rippled through her that wasn't from cold.

Fargo placed an arm around and patted her shoulder to reassure her. He conjured up things to say that might encourage her, but she kissed him before he could open his mouth.

It was an affectionate kiss at first, lazy and teasing. Then it changed, and a smoldering passion seemed to take fire in her. She pressed against Fargo, squirming and rubbing, her mouth like a bitter fruit that would give a man a pain when he tasted it. She broke her embrace as abruptly as she'd begun it, and cuddled closer. "Why not, if we're staying?" she purred.

He reached for her, weaving fingers through her hair. Why not? He was hardly in any condition to promote a great, lathering romp, but when a woman has the wants, a man finds the will. And hell, they were staying awhile.

Natasha crouched her naked body to his, kissing him with hot, moist urgency, first his lips, then the hollow of his neck, then lower to taunt his nipples. She slipped wetly along his abdomen, feeling his satiny skin ripple under her teasings. Then still lower, her lips probing and exploring as she heard Fargo moan with swelling pleasure.

Then, giving a whimpering cry, Natasha leaned over to quickly taste his rampant erection. She licked the sensitive underside of the glans. She widened her mouth to absorb its thick crown, then ovaled her lips tightly around the corona, and began dipping her head up and down. She worked her tongue. She felt Fargo stiffen harder and grow. She purred and slowed her action to a tantalizing, sensuous pumping that drew gasps from Fargo and caused his hips to rotate against her.

She raised her head, licking her lips. "Do it," she mewed, and rolled over on her hands and knees. "The ground's too hard for my back and bottom, Skye, but do it to me . . . do it as good as you did last time . . ."

Fargo positioned himself directly behind her, running his hands over the smooth cheeks of her soft buttocks. He could feel them quivering expectantly under his touch, and then he heard her moan as his aching shaft penetrated the tender lips of her upraised cleft. He felt her hand as she reached back under her body, her fingers urgently enfolding his girth, moving him up and down for a moment, parting her young flesh and guiding him gently forward.

"Ahhh," she sighed breathlessly, seeming to swallow the whole of him inside her as she slid back, impaling herself. Fargo clasped his hands tightly around her wasplike waist, gripping her while he began to stroke into her, his loins flattening her buttocks with each sawing thrust he drove into her gripping channel.

Leaning forward, Fargo shifted one hand to knead her jiggling breast, toying harshly with her nipple, while she arched up and back like a bucking bronco. Her right hand slid under her body, this time to caress Fargo's scrotum, massaging him with the lightest of touches.

Tensing, he felt the squeeze of her loins pulling at his manhood, and he plunged faster, deeper, penetrating her with all his strength. And her passage kept squeezing, squeezing, squeezing, hoarse moans keening from her slackening mouth. The squeezing became unbearable until, bursting, Fargo came in a great gush.

Natasha's clenching hips worked and sucked as if his hot seed were an invigorating tonic. Then, with a sigh of satiation, Natasha slid forward, releasing Fargo's deflating erection, her inner thighs wet and glistening in the dimness. Fargo just hunched there, feeling vanquished.

Nothing like brisk exercise to warm a man up, he thought.

As the pleasant aftermath wore thin, they turned to opening the bundle. As Fargo slid into his clothes again, the garments felt warmer than any buffalo or bear coat he had ever worn. He checked his firearms, shucking off the weathered caps over the charges in the revolver cylinder and replacing them with gleaming new ones. The breech on the Sharps was its major problem, but it appeared to be in fair condition, no worse for wear.

Soon after that, Fargo and Natasha departed the clearing. Hastening on into the wild fastness of the hills, they moved in a sweep that would eventually bring them back down to the Sanpoil and the Columbia, where their boats were hidden. They knew the Indians would soon be on the hunt again; there was nothing like bruised pride to foster dedication. But Fargo was determined not to make it easy for them, and Natasha joined to make sure they avoided open ground and skylines, clinging instead to rocks, brush, and timber. They ate what their trail provided, which wasn't much more than enough to blunt their hungers. Mostly roots, berries, and bird eggs.

With the first lightening of the eastern sky, they arrived bleary-eyed exhausted at their concealed boats. As they launched their crafts, Natasha looked across from her dugout with an expression of foreboding.

"I got a suspicion that those braves won't hunt us alone much longer. They'll go to Chief Quinnalt, blame everything on the dead leader, and if I know the chief, he'll call his other parties in on us. We'd better hie for the Nespelem and make Zashcíta before he skins us all."

"Well, if you bust out singing on the way," Fargo warned, picking up his paddle, "it'll be me who skins you on the spot, mouth first."

8

Rain was sprinkling from a cloud-hooded sky by the time Fargo and Natasha finally reached Zashcíta. Their news only added to the depressing atmosphere.

For the next couple of days it drizzled constantly, to which the free trappers paid great invective but little mind, other than to make sure their firearms were protected. The weather continued to worsen, developing into blustery showers. Thunder was rumbling in the distance when Modoc Doyle and Abel Bone returned to the hidden pocket, together with eight trappers they'd recruited from the Harts Pass and upper Methow area. Everybody mingled, a hearty reunion with surprise and relief and some introductions thrown in. One face was missing from the company, however, and after a while Modoc Doyle went and cornered Fargo at one of the fires.

"Skye, where's Brusilov?"

"His turn at lookout," Fargo replied, gesturing up the little trail that led to the front rimrock. "You look in need of a shakedown, Modoc. Here."

Gratefully Doyle accepted a mug of hot whiskey from Fargo, then squatted by the fire. "How'd you do at Fort George?"

"Wonderful," Fargo said with sarcastic disgust.

"Got a knot on my head and had my breeches pulled out of a tight lockup by sheer luck." Concisely he related the details—well, most details—of his talk with Williard Hamilton and his escape, and of his subsequent capture and flight with Natasha.

Listening, Doyle stared sourly at the ground, then looked up when Fargo was through. "I'd say there's a fair chance that Anglican and Yankee might get together. Then if Chief Quinnalt found we had Netty here, or just notioned he wanted some mountain-man hair, we'd be caught in as nasty a middle as I ever wish to see." Doyle took a slurp of whiskey and began to say more, but was cut off by an eager bellow from above.

"Doyle? You back, good! Both come, *spéshite*—hurry!"

Glancing high, they saw Brusilov gesturing from the trail to the lookout point. They leapt up, running for the foot of the trail and hurriedly climbing to where Brusilov stood waiting. The Russian promptly turned and ran toward the top, motioning to follow, and they charged after, reaching the summit a pace behind.

"You want for the fur. You want for the fight. You want for the pirating, *da?*" Brusilov pointed out over the basin. "Look!"

They peered intently through the misty veil of rain. On a wide bend of the Columbia, just west of the confluence of the Nespelem, a mass of *bateaux* and pirogues were beaching. Nearer, up the Nespelem, five Indian canoes were drifting sluggishly with the current. It was a startling yet puzzling view that didn't fit logically. Fargo and Doyle glanced perplexed at Brusilov.

"You told us," Brusilov reminded Fargo, "you threaten Anglican boss to make peace with us or he lose his fur, is so?"

Fargo nodded; he'd reported warning Hamilton more or less that.

"Then I tell you how this must be. When you left Fort George, word went to Epinard at Fort Providence that we after his fur, too. Red Jack is tricky. He knows most risk of attack when he ships furs down Stehekin River and Lake Chelan, but knows we can strike along the Columbia or even in Astoria. So, he thinks to fool us. He make short peace with Chief Quinnalt. The Klickitat come in to trouble us. And while this is so, Red Jack brings his fur up the Columbia, under our noses, takes the Clark Fork to the Blackfoot, then portage across to the Missouri."

Pondering, Fargo surveyed the panorama below. Brusilov's theory sounded farfetched, yet it explained the scene in a way that made sense with the devious, domineering nature of Red Jack Epinard. "He's smart, okay," Fargo allowed. "Just enough to outsmart himself, maybe. By my count, there are six *bateaux*, four pirogues on the Columbia. That means maybe twenty bales of fur and about forty armed Yankee trappers. Now, closer on the Nespelem, I bet in the woods back of those six canoes are more of them. Say, fifty Klickitat could be waiting for us to charge downriver at those fur boats."

"I see," Doyle growled. "A neat little trap."

Fargo grinned ferally. "Against who?"

"Why against . . ." Doyle hesitated, scanning the Nespelem basin to the Columbia. "Spank me afire, maybe we could hit those Fort Providence varmints. Might pull it off, too, if another party kept Quinnalt's braves hoppin'. Red Jack may have just outsmarted himself—"

His voice was stilled by a clap of thunder, while weak flashes of lightning crackled yonder. Rain poured. Tugging hat brims and hunching in their coats and slickers, they left the rimrock, ignoring the runoff on the path as they wended lower.

"Rain," Brusilov snorted. "Last time like this, river overflow into old channel for half a day, and our tunnel was blocked."

"It'll be wet traveling, but the storm's made for us," Fargo responded. "We can slide right in on top of them without being seen or heard."

"Lest we drown first," Doyle muttered, boots sinking in mud.

A meeting was called. The idea of a two-pronged attack was met with enthusiasm, and the command was split between Modoc Doyle and Fargo. They worked out strategies in detail while the trappers mustered arms and ammunition. Doyle took two-thirds of the men, including the trackers, and started out overland to the Yankee boats on the Columbia. A few minutes later, with Brusilov commanding Natasha to remain behind, Fargo loaded the balance of the trappers in four canoes and headed downriver.

In the midst of flashing lightning and ear-splitting peal of thunder, they engaged the fringe of Quinnalt's trap and broke for shore, weapons raging on both sides. They ran some risk, lessened by the weather, in triggering the ambush from canoes. But it was the simplest, surest method of drawing out the braves, and besides, the whole idea was to convince Quinnalt that they were a raiding party sent out to try for Epinard's furs.

The land trembled from the force of the storm. Black flared white, then swept black again. The rain cascaded from a leaden sky. Hell ripped apart there in the basin as for two hours they maintained a running, shifting battle. Finally, the trappers began to edge back as though slowly retreating under Quinnalt's pressure, then began hooking around to catch the pursuing braves in the flank.

They were filing through a grove of trees, the river momentarily out of sight, when Brusilov up ahead waved them still. They dipped for cover and waited. Brusilov slipped forward, disappeared for a couple of minutes, then eased back to where Fargo was hiding.

"Many come," he whispered.

"How many?"

"Many! You go count, you like."

"Forget it," Fargo murmured, then turned to the others. "Ready yourselves, but let them walk through. If we nail them from behind—"

Then bodies came rustling through the underbrush. Pivoting, Fargo could make out the hazy outlines of Indians swinging lances to part foliage out of their way, but in a matter of seconds they'd stumble over his men, and then the lances would be used more conventionally.

Abel Bone didn't wait for that to happen. There was the sign of hand against buckskin, then the glint of his knife arcing upward to bury itself in the nearest brave's chest. Toad-eye Topes was launching in a silencing tackle at the next in line, even as the first was flopping in a heap, gurgling quietly to himself. But Topes was an instant too late. The third brave, realizing something was amiss, gave out a spontaneous yelp, which was choked off in a neck-wrenching grip as McHugh landed atop him.

Fargo, slitting the throat of yet another brave, sensed the damage that had been done by that yell. The more braves they could drop silently, simultaneously, the better their odds against the rest. That was why he'd stabbed his victim through the side of the neck and ripped outward; the common version of slicing from ear to ear would have allowed the man one last, loud shout.

In response to the yell, the braves stretched out only yards away began surging forward en masse. The ambush began turning into a bloody melee; Fargo realized it could swiftly degenerate into total collapse. Reacting with cold instinct, he fired his Colt at the first man who rose into view, then scrambled on all fours to a safer position as his old one was chopped to bits.

Brusilov and the others were also swiveling around in crouches and blasting away with determination with their pistols, the fight too close and furious to use rifles. A second brave's face disappeared, then a third's. A fourth fell to his hips, his legs shot away at the thigh. Still others came on, spearing, clubbing, slinging darts and rocks. It looked in the cloud-burst darkness as if a horde of hundreds was descending, and Fargo wasn't sure if he hadn't seriously underestimated the size of Quinnalt's forces. Only surprise had been on their side, and now that was gone.

Continually moving, gliding among the trees, the trappers shot and stabbed the encircling Indians. Whirling, Williams neatly drilled a brave who was in the act of lancing one of the recruits from Harts Pass. Topes, diving sideways as wood splintered inches from his nose, swiveled and fired back, the acrid odor of powder dilating his nostrils. His target tripped and fell, upsetting the aim of the brave beside him, allowing Renfrew to punch a .51-caliber hole through his chest, the brave sagging in a heap over the tripped one.

With his left hand, Fargo stabbed down at a brave he'd already wounded in the side. The brave, snarling gutturally, blocked the knife with the pole of his lance, then tried to twist it around so that its blade would flip the knife out of Fargo's grasp. Fargo brought his Colt around; it clicked empty. Frantic, he lunged down against the lance pole, forcing it against the brave's throat. The man struggled with it, then let go and groped for Fargo's neck. Fargo pressed harder, hearing raspy breath, seeing the blue-mottled features writhing, mouth gaping. The brave shuddered convulsively and died.

Fargo stumbled back from the body, sickened. This was squalid brawling on the ugliest, basest level of animal survival. And still more renegades were advancing, some shouting with fury, others exultant with assured victory, if only by their numbers. Weapons tore the air as the trappers danced from spot to spot and crawled furiously through the shadowed muck.

His Colt empty and lacking the time or dry cover to reload, Fargo snatched up his dead opponent's lance and threw it at a suddenly rushing brave. The brave ducked, the lance sailing harmlessly over his head, and then, as if he were running a hurdle race, he leapt over a fallen comrade and bowled into Fargo. They struck the sodden earth, all arms and legs and gripping hands. Fargo couldn't swing up his knife or club with the otherwise useless revolver, and the soldier's weapons pouch slipped loose, swallowed by the dense, dark action of their struggle. His hard skull crunched against Fargo's jaw and raked his nose, sending blood flying. Fargo scraped his fingers in the brave's greasy hair and then brought the edge of his other hand across to pay him back in kind. There was the satisfying noise of a broken nose, and only the quick averting of his head saved the brave from having his brain pierced with slivers of bridge bone and cartilage.

The brave responded by thrusting a bony hand against Fargo's loins and wrenching at his genitals in a vicious, vicelike twist. Fargo almost blacked out as they continued rolling in a tight ball together. Only dimly did he perceive the sounds of shooting, screaming, and savage battle going on around him. His world was momentarily confined to the squeezing clutch between his legs and the searing agony spiraling up from his belly.

In desperation, Fargo yanked his arm back and poked stiffened fingers directly into the brave's eyes. He could feel the sockets warm and moist, and then the brave was falling away from him, howling. Fargo, panting, grimacing from pain, scrambled frantically up to fall upon the writhing brave, heedless of the squirming while he grabbed him by the head and broke him over his knee. Fargo severed the brave's windpipe and jugular vein with one swift gutting motion of his knife, then tried to stand. His knees gave way.

All was still when Fargo at last rose to his feet. He swayed, leaning against a tree trunk for support, tenderly massaging his crotch to see if all his equipment was still there. It felt as if half had been torn out by the roots.

Scattered around were shattered, bloodied corpses sprawled in every conceivable position. Toad-eye Topes and Ol' Williams, coughing slightly, were gingerly stepping among the fallen, making sure they were all dead. Most other trappers were squatting against trees or sitting upon rocks, some like Bone having coats over their head while they reloaded their firearms. Brusilov was slouched, holding his stomach. McHugh was spraddle-legged off to one side, taking a piss. The entire clash had taken ten minutes, if that, yet it seemed to Fargo to have stretched for an eternity. Ruefully, he had to admit it had come damn close to just that for him.

"What happened?" he asked. "How'd we do?"

"Chased them off, leastwise till they've licked their hurts. We got four dead, four injured, and McHugh," Topes replied, glancing up from one dead brave and gesturing toward the Irish trapper, who was turning, buttoning his fly.

"It's nothing," McHugh said, though the front of his face was smeared with blood. "Scalp wound is all. It's already stopped bleeding."

"Okay." Fargo eyed Brusilov. "What about you?"

"Lance pole in gut. Knocked my wind out."

"Blew a fart, he means," Renfrew said, grinning. "Gassed the poor redskins to death."

Casting a scowl at Renfrew, Fargo began marshaling the trappers to return. They had to be quick, for Quinnalt had pulled back only to regroup, he was sure, and would soon come thirsting for revenge. Leaving the dead for later burial, they patched and carried the wounded to their canoes, raced upriver, hid the craft, and tore through to Zashcíta before any Indians could close in and discover the tunnel entrance.

By this time the rain was a sullen roar, descending in solid sheets. Fargo felt a little uneasy about Doyle's party when he saw that water was already flowing through the tunnel. But when they reached Zashcíta, he found that Doyle and his crew had arrived ahead of him. The entire pocket, despite the pelting downpour, was echoing with high humor. The floor of the cabin was littered with fresh bales of fur. And under guard of a dozen eager guns, Red Jack stood captive.

Doyle came up, clapped a heavy hand to Fargo's shoulder, and ushered him over to Epinard. "You oughta hear this curly wolf howl," he exulted, "now that we pulled his teeth and got him walkin' like a duck."

"Enjoy while you can, *vous culs*," Epinard snarled. "You cannot hold me! M'sieu Teague, owner of Yankee, put me at Fort Providence because I cannot be whipped. And I cannot! There's different days coming, days when Rouge Jacques Epinard's top dog and nothing in all the northwest that don't play my music."

"Crap," Fargo said in flat scorn.

The factor's face swelled with rage. "Damn you, I will have you flayed in my compound before the fall. In two weeks M'sieu Teague comes to inspect my fort. I shall take him to see how I handle swine like you, Skye Fargo, before I tell him Providence belongs to me, not to his skinflint company."

Fargo shrugged, turning away. Still, Epinard's boasts had a ring of assurance that caused him unease. A moment later Natasha touched his arm and pointed to the area around the mouth of the tunnel. Waters were churning, filling the foot of the pocket there, backing up from the river and overflowing through the tunnel. With Natasha at his side, Fargo returned to report the news to Doyle and Brusilov, who was also by the prisoner.

"Our passage is flooded," Brusilov agreed, gazing that way.

"So we can't hold you, Red Jack? You can't get away," Doyle gloated, and cut the tight bonds restraining Epinard. "You'll be a prisoner here till we've got peace in this region, and you'll be a prisoner on a long ride to the law. Go ahead, stretch your legs if you like, while you can."

Epinard gave no answer. Freed, he strolled aimlessly toward the maelstrom churning angry, muddy foam in the craggy rocks and pool around the blocked tunnel mouth. The eyes of the camp followed him. He stood for a long moment staring into the water. Fargo saw his shoulders rise and fall as if in resignation.

Then, without warning and with a wild, derisive cry, Red Jack Epinard plunged into that deadly welter of raging water.

For a moment Fargo and the trappers stood flabbergasted. Then they broke into a pell-mell run to the water, but there was no sign of Epinard to be seen.

"Red Jack called me an asshole, and sure proved it," Doyle groaned, shaking his head dolefully. "But damn, I really thought he was stuck here."

"He was," Bone consoled. "Ain't a man could live through the tumblin' he'll get in that channel."

Topes nodded. "I guess he feared we'd treat him like a Klickitat."

"If he wanted to go that bad," Renfrew added, "let him."

"Now we won't have to feed him or post a guard," Topes said.

For all their certainty, Fargo felt troubled concerns. If somehow Epinard managed to make it outside, all hell would break loose, and the secrets of Zashcíta would be known to the enemies of the free trappers. However remote, it was a risk they couldn't afford. He swung toward the press of men and singled out Brusilov. "Pick the three men who read trail sign best. You and Modoc and I'll take them out soon's the water drops. We'll find Epinard and bury him deep."

Brusilov stared at the water. "Maybe we don't find dead man," he said softly. "Red Jack one brave fool, plenty strong, plenty big. Maybe we find only tracks, tracks going west."

The trappers chuckled, ready to dismiss Brusilov's forebodings as part of the old man's dour craziness. But Natasha cut them short.

"Listen to Papa," she pleaded. "He knows. I know. I was caught on those rocks in the last flood. He tried to reach me and was caught by the current, and went out through the tunnel. Hours later when the water was gone, he came back in, clothes torn and skinned raw, but otherwise untouched."

"Well, if Brusilov lived through . . ." Fargo cursed under his breath, surveying the trappers again. "Okay, six of us are going out either to pick up Epinard's carcass or to track him down. But he might be alive and give us the slip. We can't take any chances like him warning Hamilton, who'd recall my warning and ship his furs out as fast as

102

possible. There are some stolen free-trapper pelts on those bales, I figure, and you've got to have them. Those who aren't coming with me, drive for Fort George, grab your furs, and get back."

Wide grins creased the trappers' faces at the anticipation of striking for what was theirs. Doyle took off his sagging cap and wrung the water from it with a disgusted glance at the sky.

"I think Skye's right, boys. Have at it. Don't worry about meetin' Quinnalt's braves on the way. Epinard shot his mouth a mite to me while we was taking him in, and it seems he promised Quinnalt sixty rifles outta the Fort Providence stock for throwin' in with him. He was plumb upset we'd took him prisoner. Said nobody at his post knew about his deal, and that if Quinnalt didn't get his guns, his warriors'd go hit Providence. I got a hunch Quinnalt's already started west to do that. He couldn't find us out there, and you know how an Indian is when he thinks he's been cheated."

Fargo hoped Doyle was right. If they were forced to look very far for Epinard's body or for sign of the man, it would help matters considerably to have the woods cleared of the renegades. But time was passing, and if the Yankee factor had survived through the water, he could well be on his way west. Impatiently Fargo watched the clouds above the pocket for hints of thinning.

9

The storm raged riotously on through the night.

By dawn it had begun to subside, thunder and lightning blowing onward with their cloud-bursting head winds. The rain tapered and quit. Along about midmorning, the water receded, draining from the flooded tunnel.

Less than an hour out of Zashcíta, Brusilov and Doyle uncovered sign on the bank of the Nespelem that Red Jack Epinard had escaped death. He was apparently barefoot, likely half-naked after the pummeling of the water. Soon after, where Quinnalt had set his ambush on the river, they found a dead Indian, probably killed in the skirmish with Fargo's party. The brave had been stripped of all his gear, his moccasins, and his leggings. The sign Epinard now left behind him was of an uncommonly large and heavy Klickitat, traveling hurriedly west.

They pursued in two stout *bateaux*, each carrying two paddlers and a steersman, plus supplies for their arduous chase. The boats shot down the Nespelem and then the Columbia, miles falling behind swiftly. They remained ever on the alert, but caught no disturbance, saw no indication of either

Epinard or any other trouble, until they passed the Okanogan River.

Between the Okanogan and the confluence of the Methow was a perilous stretch of rapids. As the roar of cataracts grew in volume, they surged through the last curve, where normally they would land to portage around the deadly hazard. And there a dozen canoes were pulled up in a line, and upward of thirty long-haired, painted renegades stood staring agape, most with long bows and quivers of arrows slung across their shoulders.

The mutual surprise lasted all of a second. While the six trappers swept abreast, the braves let out a ferocious howl and loosed a flight of arrows. That fairly tore any notion of portage, Fargo knew, for if they landed, they'd never leave alive. Yet if they didn't, the gnashing thunder of those rapids lay dead ahead. The choice seemed slight, but had to be made instantly. From his stance at the foremost sweep, Fargo caught up his Sharps and triggered a slug into the body of one of the Indians.

"Drive on," he roared.

The Indians were leaping to their light craft, shoving into the current. The trappers, echoing Fargo's order, were bending to the paddles, steering away from the bank and into the first pull of the rapids. Another flight of arrows whipped out at them, but the range was long and the men paid no heed, too busy to fire back.

The current grabbed the boats, whirled them down into the torrent. The lighter craft of the Indians fell behind, held by back strokes, as their crews stared in wonderment at the foolhardy whites who would shoot the rapids. The Klickitats were soon blotted from sight by flying spume as great waves shattered against sawtoothed rocks.

Fargo, beaten by the haft of his sweep, shouted orders as he peered ahead through sheets of spray.

Snatches of those orders echoed back to Doyle, steersman of the second boat, who bellowed them to his crew. Chill water drenched them. Their muscles cramped from the punishment. The faint call of Doyle's booming voice caused Fargo to wonder how the second craft was faring, but he dared not look. Even the slight digression of thought sent his boat shuddering, leaping like a bird and slamming back to the water, bottom down, in a series of bumping jounces. He felt the tremble as a fang of stone planed off a long, curling shaving the entire length of one gunwale, and frantically strove to guide the yawing boat clear, only to smash against another jagged outcrop and ricochet off the next.

On they raced, battling, scraping over corrugated bedrock, and crunching against projections, the glancing jolts causing the wooden craft to creak and almost buckle. Finally, lurching, all but foundering, they careened into calmer water and floated with the carrying tide, the crew hanging limp over the gunwales while they recovered their strength.

Upon reaching the Methow, they turned up the tributary and paddled against current for almost twenty-five miles to Libby Creek. They couldn't go far along the Libby and shortly beached their craft in the flanking foothill thickets. There was another reason they chose here to pull in—an abandoned Indian canoe wedged in the bank. Minutes later they located prints like those Epinard had left back at the Nespelem, and nobody doubted that the sign belonged to the Fort Providence factor.

Their discovery came as no wild shock. The trappers and Epinard both knew the territory well, and not surprisingly would pick much the same route to Fort Providence. At this point they were on a direct line between Zashcíta and the Yankee fur post, which overlooked Stehekin River where it widened into Lake Chelan. It would have required an eighty-mile loop to reach Fort Providence via the Columbia, but from here it was a straight shot overland across the Sawtooth Ridge—well, almost straight; in order to skirt the 8,800-foot Oval Peak, they decided to angle up and over to Prince Creek, which flowed down the western flank of the Sawtooths to Lake Chelan.

By the tracks, Epinard too had chosen to take the minor detour. Without equipment, certainly stiff and battered after his experience, the big factor astonished Fargo by managing to hold a lead. The days-old chase lasted days more, deep up timbered breaks and clefts to the jagged spires outlined against the sky, then down from the summits through dense, steeply angled groves. Once they began following Prince Creek lower, the trappers as often as not were hemmed in by a combination of trees, ravines, and cliffs for almost its entire tumbling course to Lake Chelan. There, from the bordering woods, the creek wound sluggishly, joining other streams, shallow puddles, and brackish ponds rivuleting across the soggy ground in trickles.

Along the shoreline ran a crude wagon trail, connecting the settlement at the south of the lake to Fort Providence, a dozen miles northwest. In the trail's churned-earth ruts were the telltale imprints of Red Jack Epinard. Seeing them, the six weary men who had dogged the grim red ghost all this distance called a rest break, glumly aware they had lost the race. Most likely Epinard was already back at his fort, but even if not, they had no real hope of catching up with him in time. If they tried, they'd undoubtedly be spotted out along the trail, which was wide open to view from ahead, behind, and the lake. Their only remaining chance to thwart Epinard—slim as it might be—rested on the element of surprise. Should Epinard or his crew become forewarned, the difficult task would become virtually impossible.

Tired, faces somber, Fargo and the trappers sprawled on a mossy spot at the treeline by Prince Creek. There they were out of casual sight from the trail and lake, and a ridge ran along above them, sheltering their position from the higher ground beyond. For a quarter of an hour they crouched talking—until suddenly Abel Bone rolled to his belly and swiftly fired his rifle upslope, snapping out a curse.

"Damn! Two of 'em! Drop 'em afore they get away and give warning."

It happened fast. Fargo pivoted in time to glimpse two men's figures in full silhouette on the crest of the ridge. One of them wavered and vanished on the heels of Bone's hasty shot. His shout and a fusilade of rifle fire roared the next instant, the second man falling forward and collapsing flat, unmoving.

Fargo waved away the powder smoke. "We get them?"

Doyle sprang to his feet, shaking his head. "Dunno," he growled, and started running up the slope. The other trappers and Fargo bounded after him. They crested the rise three hundred yards from where they had been resting, close to where the second man lay riddled, facedown. There was also a wet scarlet blotch on the grass and blood-dripped tracks leading away into a covert of timber.

Bone swore bitterly. "Spyin' on us! Damn Epinard an' his wolves!"

"Damn Pierre Vaurien, y'mean, Abel." Doyle responded, having turned over the dead man. He stood frowning, scratching his hair. "Don't you recollect this guy? He's one of Vaurien's rebel Canucks."

The trappers crowded, peering, and chorused agreement.

"What's he doin' here?" Toad-eye Topes asked.

"Question is, what's Vaurien up to," Fargo replied thoughtfully, shaking his head. "The other man could answer that, but no use trying to follow him. He's got a start and knows where he's going. He'd skin away from us."

Brusilov spat. "So what we do now?"

"I'd say keep on. We cut off the trail and sneak around through the trees to Fort Providence like we figured, like this never happened. Vaurien may have located us, but if he's not tied in with Epinard somehow, Epinard wouldn't necessarily know what we intend, and we could still surprise him."

"Sounds okay," Doyle conceded. "Only one thing wrong with it, Skye."

"What?"

"That 'if' . . ."

From the ridge, they plunged through timber in a northwesterly direction. The forest was a trackless swath of mature conifers, uniformly sized and widely spaced, rising straight and branchless to great heights before their crowns unfurled. At times the imposing stand softened into a landscape of average groves, stone ledges, and rough fields, where birds could be heard chattering from bowers. But once back under the high canopy of trees, there was silence.

As the afternoon waned, they heard noise of labor and came upon a logged-off acreage. In the middle of the clearing stood a simple, square log cabin with an adjoining corral and the foundation of a barn nearby. About a quarter of the way around the clearing, a stolid young settler in coveralls and caulk boots was sawing through a large Douglas fir.

When the settler saw them approaching, he stiffened defensively.

"Howdy," Fargo called affably. "Just passing through, friend."

"So did the last pack, after chowin' me outta vittles."

"Last pack? They looked like us?"

"Looked like trappers," the settler hedged, and began cutting again, trying to cold-shoulder his visitors as they drifted in around him.

"Where're they going?" Doyle queried.

"Fort Providence, I assume. Ain't y'all?"

Fargo's lips quirked. By his disgruntled manner and tone, the settler had received roughshod treatment from those frequenting the post, which might prove a help now. "We're not Yankee fur men. And the only way we want to get to the fort is unseen. Is it possible?"

"I reckon, by skirting through the flats." The settler's expression remained grudging, but his eyes mirrored dawning realization. "You don't mean to steal into the fort, do you?"

Fargo shrugged; the trappers said nothing.

"But . . . but just y'all against ten times your number?"

"Of the best?"

"Ah, well, when are those left holding a fort ever the best?" The settler gave a smirk for a moment, then clamped serious again. "But they aren't asleep neither. You'll never make it."

"It can be tried. That is, if nobody rats."

"Not me, not a breath! However, seein' as how I live so close an' buy my supplies there, listen up . . ." The settler leaned into his sawing with heavy strokes as he described the structure and routine of the fort. When at last he was finished, he gazed up at the creaking fir while he said to Fargo, "I wish I could do more, but now you must go, quickly."

"Yankee men?"

"The tree. It's fixing to fall where y'all stand."

Everyone swiveled; the fir teetered. Swiftly retreating, they felt the rush of air and heard the crack of wood, the trunk splitting from its stump and hammering flat the spot where they'd been gathered. Its quake was still reverberating as they ducked back into timber and headed toward the lake.

Presently they hiked down through a grove to the flats, as the settler had called them. It was more akin to a wide, brackish estuary off the lake, a slough of cattails and mud. The ground was a shimmery paste as they descended, the turgid undergrowth murky from dusk drawing low, and the farther they slogged across the marshland, the darker and deeper a menace it became.

They struggled between waxy stalks and huge dead trees, thrashing at greedy insects that whined perniciously. The trappers were forced to wade through viscid gumbo that clung with each step, and to weasel through tall nettling grasses and slimy plants, occasionally snagging on sunken limbs or hidden roots. And though the men felt their bearing was correct, their sense of direction grew increasingly blurred, becoming as distorted and mired as their course. They could only plug on, hoping their faith in the settler's advice was founded on a firmer basis than this muck.

Gradually the festering swamp began to thin out, just as had been described it should. The morass was slowly broadening, diluting, eventually forming a delta that opened to the shore. Ahead was the soft-lapping Lake Chelan, pallid dimness sifting high toward a clouded twilight.

Exhausted, the six crossed the remaining shoals and earthen banks, coming to the end of their serpentine trek. The lake rolled south into an unbroken meld with an opaque horizon, and north to the mouth of Stehekin River. To their immediate right was a shallow cape, mounded by the high-walled Fort Providence, which blocked the sickly eventide and was suffused by thin wreathing mists.

Permeating the shoreline was a clabbered bog. The entire bank driveled in a lengthy strand along both sides of the delta inlet, rising denser to thick inland hillocks, but sweeping molten out around to the borders of the promontory.

"Now, do we slink along the shore?" Doyle asked.

"We'd be too visible," Fargo answered. "No, we've got to try climbing that first small ridge at the neck of the cape, so we can check what's what. Don't forget, the settler thought he'd overheard plans to patrol out around the fort."

McHugh sighed fervently. "Whatever he thinks, I'll believe."

They started to file cautiously along the ribboned shelf that ran like a barely submerged sandbar across one side of the inlet. It drained away before they could reach a landward edge, leaving them stuck with no other spot to jump to. They had to swim the remaining narrow channel, struggling through entangling weeds. Then, crawling onto a slippery dune of the nearest hummock, they darted furtively toward the cape's neck until they could delve back into the cover of surrounding foliage. The rest of the way they forged through the perpetual dimness of old-growth timber, avoiding thickets and keeping to the sound-deadening carpet of needles as much as possible, and finally emerging onto an open ledge of stunted brambles and shrubbery.

They had reached the slope overlooking the fort.

From the cape's ridged neck, they surveyed the enclosed post laid out just a few simple yards below. Providence, built squat and thick and square-lined, was ugly in its strength, with loopholed firing benches and sentry boxes atop its stout palisades.

Lamplight glowed within, the arched main gate was shut, and men could be glimpsed at firing posts along the front. Obviously the Yankee factor had returned and anticipated pursuit, although nothing showed he knew when to expect an assault. It could be reasonably assumed, too, that having reached his base with information as to the force and location of the free trappers, Epinard would immediately begin scheming to wipe them out.

To stop him were six armed fighters, the old element of surprise, and a certain degree of complacency. The fort seemed so safe that it helped lull attentiveness. No, the Yankee defenders were far from asleep, Fargo thought as he recalled the settler's warning, but they weren't as awake as they should have been either.

"Looks solid as a prison," McHugh grumbled. "By the Holy Virgin, it sure smites against my grain to try breaking *into* jail."

"Plus back out," Fargo said. Then catching some of the trappers' dubious expressions, he added, "Sometimes it works out the fewer there are, the better the chances."

Doyle sighed. "Nothing times nothing still equals nothing . . ."

Crimson and violet streaked the horizon. Like a wound, Fargo thought as they waited for darkness— like a festering wound. While he tried to calculate their approach, analyzing the fort for points of weakness, he had a sapling cut back in the timber and notched along its length to serve as a crude scaling ladder. Finally the last rays flickered and died, extinguished below the rim of mountains to the west and replaced by a starless, swarthy night.

"Here goes nothing," Fargo said, straightening in the darkness.

He led the trappers down the cape's brushy slope.

From the ridgeline, an expansive open field stretched to the palisade far to one side of the neck. Everywhere else, however, particularly the front of the cape and the sections closer to the main gate, was more strongly defended, since anywhere else was a more logical site to attack. A flanking maneuver such as theirs was evidently considered too impractical and hazardous, a blatant folly that everyone was allowing everyone else to guard against. Or so Fargo was hoping when he'd chosen the route.

The trappers began snaking through the waist-high grass, wary in case the the fort's outer perimeter was under patrol, as the settler had warned. They were spread out to lessen the risk of a concentrated movement being spotted, with Toad-eye Topes at the end nearest the lake's edge. Abruptly he vanished from sight. At the same instant, a man called out in a voice more curious than suspicious.

Signaling the others down, Fargo and Doyle crept sideward, knives in hand. The man called again, louder and more querulous. Suddenly his voice was choked off, followed by a soft scuffling noise.

Breaking out of the grass alongside the bank, Fargo and Doyle saw Topes pressing close behind the man, seemingly holding him up by the neck. The man was clad like a Yankee trapper, his fur cap tipped askew along with his head, his boots dancing on the rocky soil, while he shuddered convulsively in Topes' grip—and then hung slack.

Topes released him, having throttled him swiftly and efficiently. He simply hadn't known the man was not alone. What the two other Yankee fur men were silently doing along the shoreline was anyone's guess, but before the body had fallen, before Topes fully released him, the pair was leaping in attack. Unaware their comrade was dead, they were trying to rescue the man, wrestling him upright while they pistol-whipped Topes.

Topes was struggling down on his knees when Fargo and Doyle charged into the fight. One of the fur men kicked Topes in the head, then pivoted to aim at Fargo. But Fargo was closing too fast with his knife, and the man only had time to block Fargo's thrust with his gun arm. Fargo parried and was curving his knife back underneath the man's arm for another stab at his target when Doyle skewered his own blade up under the man's ribs and then cut him open all the way to his breastbone. Blood and guts mushroomed out everywhere, the man toppling backward, mouth and eyes wide open. Springing aside to avoid the gush, Fargo glanced to where Topes was dispatching the other fur man by using his knee and a necklock to break the man's spine. There was a crack, and the man dropped.

The others rushed up from the grass, where they had been covering the action. They would have fired if it had come to that, but had purposely held back, none of them wanting to risk the noise. Quickly they took the arms and legs of the dead fur men and carted them down the bank to the lake, where they eased them into the water and let them sink.

Hastening on then, they burrowed across the field to the rear palisade of the fort. Throwing their sapling against the log wall there, the trappers waited breathlessly while Fargo worked agilely up its springy length to check the other side.

The makeshift ladder was not quite tall enough, but with a final flexing of muscle, Fargo shinnied to the rough-cut crown of the wall. His fingers spidered on the log ends as he balanced himself, bringing up his legs to crouch catlike on his toes. Before he could properly set himself, he glimpsed the outline of a man pacing between the wall and a nearby shed. The man sauntered lethargically, idly toting a Short Pattern Enfield carbine as he approached where

Fargo shifted delicately overhead, motioning a warning to the trappers. A splinter of wood snapped beneath Fargo; the sound was faint, but it was enough. The man glanced upward. Fargo pounced.

The man tried defending himself, but it was too late. He raised his carbine, but Fargo smashed it aside as he landed on him, both knees directly in the gut. He tore the gun away, reversed it, and bashed the stock against the side of the man's head. The man grunted, fell over, and lay comatose.

"André!"

A man's voice, deep and gravelly, came from around the side of the shed. Fargo dived for cover behind a support pillar, leaving the first man exactly as fallen, minus his carbine.

"André?"

The second man trotted into view—the patrol buddy, Fargo surmised, attracted by the scuffle. He glanced around, not immediately spotting his partner. Fargo hefted the carbine by its twenty-four-inch barrel.

"*André!*"

The second man ran to the body, kneeling to see what he could do. "Whatsa matter, pal? Too much o' that puky wine we—"

Fargo's swing caught the guard above the temple. The man had time for a gentle gasp, his eyes rolling up to stare quizzically at Fargo, before lapsing unconscious. Fargo dragged him to the pillar and propped him so he appeared to be slouching asnooze, hauled the first man to join him, then chucked a rock over the wall as an all-clear signal.

"Ow! Shit!" he heard faintly. A moment later, the trappers scaled the wall one by one and leapt to the ground, the last to climb the ladder kicking it down after him. They paused to regroup, Doyle handing Fargo his Sharps, McHugh grimacing as he rubbed the top of his head, and then they began to steal belly-low toward the rear of the main building, advancing in circuitous stages, dipping from shed to barn, smithy to warehouse, continually on the lookout for Epinard's cutthroat fur men.

Reaching the corner of the structure across from the main building, they drew in and listened, scanning the area. Fronted by a wide, packed-earth yard, the building served as the trade store, company offices, and the factor's private quarters. Toward the rear of one side, they spotted a recessed door with a tiny stoop and a tinier overhang. There were no other doors, and the few windows were of oiled hide, small-paned, impossible to go through noiselessly.

Again Fargo went first, alone. Darting to the side door, he crouched with senses keen, but saw nothing outside nor heard anything from within. Not surprisingly, the door proved to be locked. Hunkering down on the stoop, he opened the bone-handled pocket clasp knife he'd borrowed from Toad-eye Topes. Known as a *navaja*, its single six-inch blade was the thinnest and most pliant of the steel carried by the trappers, and as hoped, it slid easily between the doorjamb and faceplate. Levering and picking, he cautiously snicked back the latch bolt and pushed the door.

Satisfied, he motioned to the trappers and eased inside. They came in a flying wedge, the last to enter shutting the door quietly behind him. As their eyes adjusted to the darkness, they found that they were standing in a large pantry. Directly ahead was a double-doored entry to a kitchen. The kitchen was unoccupied, though its clutter of foodstuffs and utensils showed that it was in constant use. On their left, a long corridor extended to a closed door. Up on the wall beside the door was a whale-oil bracket lamp, its low flame supplying the corridor's only illumination.

Returning the clasp knife to Topes, Fargo gently slid the double doors shut and padded with the trappers up the dimly lit corridor. He made it even dimmer, reaching out and lowering the wick of the bracket lamp, then flattened against the closed door, listening. The trappers hovered, tensely hushed.

Talk filtered through, muffled but understandable.

10

From the settler's descriptions, Skye Fargo knew the room beyond was the factor's private office. It adjoined the trade store, from which could be heard low, soft murmurs of business, like background noise for the sharp parley in the office.

"So we fight together," Epinard's unmistakable voice was saying, "the Anglican for Great Britain, Rouge Jacques for La Belle France—"

"France!" The outburst had a gruff, sardonic tone that sounded vaguely familiar; it took Fargo a moment to identify the speaker as Yankee Fur's owner, Ulysses Teague. "France hasn't been important in the West since the Louisiana Purchase."

"Ahh," Epinard sighed, and a chair squeaked as if he were gesturing eloquently. "France is very far away. So I shall be France, here in America. *Vous comprenez?*"

"I understand many things. You're a two-tongued viper making an outlaw post of Fort Providence. You're not content to just betray me, you're seeking to snare Will Hamilton into the web of your mad scheme—*ugh!*"

Along with Teague's painful groan, there came a meaty crunch like a fist striking flesh, a horrified gasp high-pitched enough to be a woman's, and the dull thump of a chair toppling over, followed by the crisp British accent of Leon Ives. "Hold your tongue, you blighter, or you'll find your face tied up like your arms and legs."

"Listen to the banty rooster," Epinard chortled. "Hear him crow, eh? One would think he's *chef* and you his hireling, M'sieu Hamilton. But, no, it's only you who's as good as me and fit to be my partner."

"Aye, we're together, Red Jack. I've been patient and long-suffering, but that's no longer a virtue," Williard Hamilton asserted, his voice like the whetting of a scythe. "Between us, I swear, we'll eradicate those murdering free trappers and prevent any more such fur brigands from slinking in."

Before Hamilton finished, Fargo heard a tart interruption, "It won't do, Father," and he recognized the snappish voice as Celeste's. "Striking in with him and risking carnage would ruin company prestige and your own reputation. Why, the man's unscrupulous. He can't be trusted not to turn on you, like he has already on Mr. Teague."

"Celeste, you know Epinard acted out of necessity. Teague's refused to cooperate, and there are jackals loose amongst us. We must unite in destroying them, else they'll bloody well drive us out and ransack what's ours."

"M'selle Hamilton, the game is larger than you believe. At stake is the big, rich Northwest, long coveted and occupied by rival nations, most recently as a territory of Les États-Unis—a hollow claim, based on the specious Oregon Treaty and backed by a faraway army. *Voilà*, your father and I, we sweep the American south and east, push the Russe west into the sea, win this land again for France and Britain. Friends, allies, we shall hold it

120

together. It's a great prize I offer . . ."

Listening to Epinard, exchanging glances with the incredulous trappers, Fargo marveled at the factor's seeming change of character. Instead of a bellicose Canuck killer, he suddenly sounded like an impassioned French patriot. And though his intention to reestablish France in the New World struck Fargo as an insane lost cause, in the process he and his mongrel crew, teamed with the vindictive Anglican men, could wreak considerable havoc and terror, perhaps even take over temporarily.

"Few men who live can offer so much to their flag," Epinard was declaring. "Remember this, *mam'selle*, when you scourge Rouge Jacques—"

His spiel choked off abruptly, as a noisy racket of shouts and gunfire erupted from somewhere out by the front of the fort. Then above the swelling tumult erupted a fusillade of heavier rifles and a piercingly strident outcry. Fargo chilled, the hair on his neck prickling. There could be no mistaking that fearsome cry; it was the Klickitat war whoop.

Someone rapped and rushed in the other door, the hubbub from the trade store loud in the office till he slammed the door shut. "Quinnalt's here. Musta brung his whole danged mob," a man reported, breathless and agitated. "I mean, I'm talking Injuns out there, harrying the walls, sieging the main gate. Still, we'd trim their wicks no trouble if them long guns didn't hold us to cover."

"Rifles? How'd they get . . . ? *Bien!* They had to've taken the rifles of the free traders, is how, after wiping them out to the very last *maudit*."

"Naw, it's trappers what's usin' the big bores."

"Free trappers and renegades? They're mortal enemies! *C'est impossible*," Epinard snapped, his chair creaking as if he were springing up. "Let's go! We've many hides to skin, eh? Leon, help M'sieu Teague out."

There was a brief flurry of bootsteps and voices while Epinard ushered everyone from his office into the clamorous trade store. Any moment now, Fargo expected Epinard to close the door and perhaps lock it after him, and in readiness, the Trailsman had his hand firm on the hall doorknob. The trappers had their hands firm on their guns. They were wound tight, every instinct insisting they cut and run. But considering the hullabaloo out there, with Yankee throngs on this side of the stockade and a swarming tribe on the other, they were not light about leaving. Besides, they'd come this far. Just ahead was Epinard's office and adjacent private quarters, begging to be searched, and sooner or later Epinard would return. Maybe he'd beg, too.

So there they were tensing with bated breath, poised to move swiftly, when Epinard ordered, "No, the other door, Lloyd. Take her by the back hall."

"I'll take me," they heard Celeste counter, "out the front."

"Don't try my patience, *chérie*. There isn't time to waste."

"Either I behave or I'm trussed up like Mr. Teague, is that it?"

"Your safety is my responsibility, your comfort is your concern."

"Oh, bullshit. You're practically holding me hostage. Why?"

"*Sécurité*." Epinard replied, derisive. "You're too much the willful goose to see the wisdom when it faces you. I can't do with you like I'd do with my *voyageurs*. I can't send you out into the hills on your own trap lines to survive or die. You're to be sheltered from hard truth and harder consequences, for you're M'sieu Hamilton's beloved *enfant*. But there's your value, too. You're the woman in your father's house, and unfortunately, his house has bats in the attic. He needs you. If something hap-

122

pen to you, it could go bad for him. Say he got mulish, like he does, without your influence he might have a mishap. So I protect you. And working together, we save your father from harm."

"A woman is a poor tool for a man waging war, Red Jack."

"*Au contraire*, she's the best!" Epinard laughed his scorn of her warning as he stepped out the door, closing it behind him.

Fargo grinned wryly. Unwittingly, Celeste and Epinard had just proven her to be right, for their brief exchange, caused by her balking, had given the trappers time to slip down the hall to the pantry. Fargo alone remained up by the door. Holding his Sharps away from bumping the wall, he stretched his other hand to extinguish the hall bracket lamp, and heard the man called Lloyd say, "C'mon, lady, you stay with me, out of trouble, in the kitchen."

Lloyd was the one who'd burst in earlier, Fargo surmised, pausing for a last glance down the hall. The trappers eyed him nervously, geared to storm outside the instant he messed up. As well he might. He'd have to grab Celeste without raising any stir, but he'd no idea how Lloyd would be armed or how he'd be gripping Celeste when he came through the door. He'd have no help; there wasn't the space for a gang-up, aside from the noise. He'd have to avoid killing Lloyd out of deference to Celeste. But worse, he had no idea how she would react. Hell, she might even refuse to be snatched.

Sucker odds, Fargo thought, grinning confidently at the trappers. Then he smothered the lamp, pinching the wick of its faint-burning flame, and the corridor was plunged into utter blackness.

"You won't find it bad, y'know," Lloyd remarked, pausing to open the door. "There's scads to eat and"—the door flung wide—"a bottle of rye in the cupboard. Judas, the lamp's fizzled. You carry any kinda spark, lady?"

The next instant Lloyd got more than he reckoned on. Fargo, shrouded in dark, could see them clearly by the glow of the office lantern, Celeste framed in the doorway, Lloyd close behind at her shoulder, a loose-limbed fidgeter with a faceful of whiskers and a handful of an Adams .44 revolver. Figuring he'd get just one crack at Lloyd—and it wouldn't be easy at best—Fargo waited only for him to glance away for more than a second.

Lloyd obliged, looking at Celeste while asking for the spark.

When Celeste answered, "A flint, maybe," and started to check, Lloyd continued focusing on her. But by then Fargo was in motion. At the last instant, Celeste caught a fleeting peripheral glimpse of blurred shadows vaulting from black depths; Fargo, on alert for this, saw her eyes bulging and her mouth widening to scream, and prayed she'd choke on it two more seconds.

One second more it took for him to reach the doorway, leaping out of the hall with his Sharps gripped lengthwise by its barrel. Celeste was still mute. Lloyd was turning to stare, gawp-faced, while reflexively bringing up his Adams .44 to aim at Fargo.

Lloyd was fast, but not as fast as a second—the extra second Fargo needed to close, ramming the Sharps past Celeste's head and smashing its metal butt plate into his throat and lower jaw with a spearing thrust. Gagging hoarsely, Lloyd snapped backward, dropping his revolver and staggering away from Celeste. Fargo sprang after, shoving by Celeste and diving into the office, flattening Lloyd with a combination of rifle butt to the face and a hard heel to the balls.

Lloyd reeled, stumbling hunched over, blood dribbling from his blanched face, incapable of even whimpering. Fargo pursued to finish it. Before he could, Lloyd put his own end to it. Blindly lurching around Epinard's desk, he blundered into a commode side table against the wall. The side table tilted, and he tripped on the suddenly exposed chamberpot. The whole works toppled on its side, the commode fracturing, the chamberpot spilling, and Lloyd sprawling limply, unconscious.

Before Lloyd hit the floor, Fargo was racing across the office.

His two seconds were past, of course, but Celeste had yet to utter a peep. She remained agape at the doorway, and by her mixed expression, she was either too dumbfounded to scream or too disconcerted to raise a squawk before finding out what's going on. But there wasn't time to fool, not after Lloyd's rowdy-dow with the commode.

Fargo snapped one terse order at the white face before him, "Grab the tail of my jacket and stick behind me. Quick!"

"My father!" Celeste cried.

There was no time to talk. A pity; naturally she worried about her father, though making him her first concern seemed overly doting. Fargo let it drop; there was no time to think. *"Quick!"* He snapped the single word once more, so forcefully, in a tone brooking no argument, that Celeste wilted and clutched her hands around the lower back of his buckskin jacket.

Entering the hallway, Fargo paused to shut the door, then plunged on down the black abyss corridor. Celeste clung to his coattail, struggling to keep pace while Fargo kept on his headlong groping toward the pantry, skimming his way along the corridor wall. Ahead, Doyle could be heard muttering curses as he fumbled open the outside door. The door was nearly wrenched off its hinges by the wedge of trappers all trying to barge outside at the same time.

With Celeste still tripping along behind, Fargo followed the trappers dashing across the open space and along the side of a storehouse. They paused at the rear corner to catch their breath, McHugh grumbling Celtic curses at Fargo for their stay in the pantry.

" 'Twas blacker'n ash buds in the front o' March," he averred.

"But lit up by the whites of your eyes, I bet," Fargo rejoined, which garnered him a few smiles from the men while he turned to Celeste. She was looking at the trappers, and she was looking appalled. Rubbing his beard, Fargo had to admit that after days of wildwood chase, they did resemble scurvy dregs, and the swamp hadn't made them smell any too sweet, either. "You can trust them, Celeste, take my word on it. I'll tell you more later, but first we've got to get away from here. Grab my jacket now and don't let go."

Celeste obeyed, eyeing him querulously. "You must be mad."

"I feel mad." Fargo set off with the trappers in a general retracing of their steps toward the rear, avoiding the post force, whose attention was still held by the firing along the front. As they faded along building to building, it became abundantly clear that fighting raged around the entire perimeter of the palisade. Indians in sorties were probing one spot, then another, testing for weaknesses while trying to weaken. The sentries at the watch boxes were constantly having to drop to the inside, run toward the next flare-up. As a result, on occasion some watch boxes were left unoccupied for a few minutes. A few minutes is all they needed. That, and a lot of luck.

A spiraling pillar of flame shot up from one of

the log cabins across the compound. A shrill cry of *"Fire!"* sheared through the air, drawing defenders from the barricades. There was a rush of men toward the leaping blaze, men who kicked the burning logs away from the bed of coals, who trampled those coals into the earth. A pall settled, darkening the night, and smoke swirled thickly across the compound. Somewhere a man's death scream rang out as an arrow found his throat. Some of the fire fighters began hastening back to fighting Indians, two of them angling by just as Fargo, Celeste, and the trappers swept around the corner of the fleshing shed.

Brusilov, snarling, triggered a shot with his pistol over Fargo's shoulder. Fargo reversed for the shed at a full run, Celeste fighting to keep her feet at that gait. Glancing back, Fargo saw the second Yankee fur man staggered by Toad-eye Topes' slug only an instant before he loosed a shot at Celeste's back.

Circling again, Fargo and Celeste came out from the fleshing shed to join the trappers. They ran swiftly on, eyes raised for any empty watch boxes or firing benches. As luck would have it, all were occupied. On a firing bench across the compound, Red Jack Epinard could be seen standing at its head, issuing frantic commands to stop what was apparently a charge against the walls and main gate. Even from their distance, Fargo and the trappers could see the stout timbers slowly giving away.

As they passed the post's forge, Fargo snatched up a woods ax. Under cover of boiling smoke from the extinguished fire, they wheeled and plunged back toward the walls. They hit opposition along the way, Yankee men firmly convinced they were Indian-siding trappers from outside. A man angling in to block passage doubled and went down, Doyle leaping over his body, smoke curling from his hip-fired rifle. Hauling Celeste along, Fargo strained to keep up with the pack. Dust stung his face from a rifle ball a scant yard away. The tail of Abel Boone's shirt, within arm's length of his head, was shredded by a howling slug. Toad-eye Topes was a little ahead, and he was waving his arm in a hurry-up gesture when his chest dissolved in a pink froth. He shriveled earthward, lying sightless with eyes staring wonderingly.

Ducking a shower of rifle fire, they left Topes where he lay, and dashed on for the walls. For a long instant Fargo ran with the clammy fear he would feel the jolt of lead tearing into the body of the woman running behind him. To have Celeste in with the free trappers—whether she wished to be or not—would be some coup and a big chip in the game. But it was not worth her life.

Reaching the wall, Fargo raced along the stockade, his hands brushing the upright tree trunks of which it was fashioned. When he came to two smaller than the rest and set together, he swung his ax. The wood seemed backed by iron, but he hacked away at a fast, steady rhythm.

Watching alongside, Celeste remarked snippily, "Well, if I were you, I'd give this up and go weasel out the way I weaseled in. I'm not you, thank heavens. I don't have to flee, and don't think you can browbeat me into joining you."

Fargo ignored her, concentrating on his chopping.

She blew now, berating, "I know that silence! I won't be fooled, Skye Fargo, not by you again. Father is so right. And Epinard too, the cad. So save your lies, I won't be gulled into going along. I flatly refuse to be a root-hog squaw, groveling lice out of your beard in some squalid camp of renegade trappers and renegade Indians, and God only knows which are worse."

"Don't fret," I'm not asking. I'm stating that you're flat wrong, except on the Indians. Your dad's wrong. Epinard's wrong and a crook, to boot. The renegade whites aren't free trappers, they're outlaws, a rogue gang kicked out at the rendezvous." Great chips flew from his lightning strokes, but the hole he was making grew slowly. "You're going. No lie, no threat, I'm not Epinard. Fact is, if he wins or if the renegades win, your life here would be on borrowed time."

The air was suddenly rent with a vast explosion as the Fort Providence powder house detonated from a flaming arrow. A volcanoing flow of incandescent flame geysered to the heavens. The blast knocked half the fort's defenders off their feet. Orders were shouted, counterorders were outshouted, and in that pandemonium, their course of action was mired in confusion.

Fargo savored the chaos. They had been lucky so far, overlooked by Indian sorties, passed unnoticed by preoccupied fur men. But he still lacked inches of being through the wall, and luck grows fickle when driven, as they'd done. At any instant someone could see his winking ax, and death would be brutal. That risk still remained, but now the odds against it had blown sky-high. Encouraged, he laid into the ax, sweat pouring from him, breath coming in great sobs. His arms were lead, but then a quick, strong hand tore the ax from his grip and sent it smashing with renewed vigor against the wood.

"And you're welcome to it, McHugh," Fargo declared, thanking the trapper. While he had the chance, then, he talked with Celeste. He couldn't tell how much she believed—if any—but as he sketched some of the highlights, it was intriguing to see her brows raise in involuntary surprise at this, and with a shade of old aversion at that. But it soon faded.

Within a very few minutes the hole was through.

Celeste did not go peaceably. She twisted angrily

in Fargo's grip as he brought her to the opening. "Oh, you're mad, you are!"

"Not as your dad." He doubled her forward and fed her through the hole, felt himself thrust roughly after her. Outside, Doyle straightened beside him.

"I got one of 'em, Skye, grab the gal's other hand. And run, run like hell for the ridge."

Fargo sucked in a great breath. Then, dragging Celeste between them, they broke from shelter, the other trappers surging right along.

Withering salvos chased them from the walls. Almost at the same instant, as though on command from one of their number, Quinnalt's warriors charged the fort in a converging attack. In their vanguard, howling as loud as any savage, Pierre Vaurien was leading his gang of outlaw Canucks. The escaping band found themselves in a whirlwind of blazing crossfire as they raced across the open field in reaching strides. Brusilov went down, his body so buffeted by flying lead that it seemed he must be riddled like a sieve. Abel Bone lost the joint of one finger to a bullet. Another slug struck McHugh, furrowing wickedly across his thigh, breaking his stride but not crippling him.

The gate gave way with a crash then and renegades poured into Fort Providence. As smoke and flames and close-quarter fighting erupted within, rifle fire no longer pursued those trying to escape. Fargo and Doyle hauled Celeste to the wooded fringe and flung down behind cover, Bone and McHugh loping brokenly for another couple of yards to find shelter. Brusilov lay motionless until the others were safe, then roaring like a stung bull, he surged to his feet and rocked on to join them. He was bleeding from the neck, the chest, and the forearm, but he seemed oblivious to his wounds. Fargo tried to twist the collar of his shirt across the gouge in his neck, but Brusilov brushed his hand away.

"Let be," he growled. "A good man don't fight till he let blood. They not hurt me yet. It can wait for Netty to tend when we get back."

A startled cry came from Celeste as she glanced up from bandaging Bone's injured hand. "Look! Over by the landing."

They looked. Heading toward the fort's lakeside dock could be seen the figures of Williard Hamilton and his subfactor, Leon Ives. Hamilton was acting reluctant—as if unwilling to leave without Celeste, Fargo thought—but Ives was determinedly forcing him to flee for the pirogues there, left tied afloat and unguarded by the victory-rash Indians. Almost to the landing they remained in view, lighted by the flames licking high over the fort.

Even more fully, the blaze outlined Red Jack Epinard atop the fiery main building in the fort. At the edge of its burning roof, above a compound packed with renegade braves, he crouched shooting one after another of a stack of guns into the press below. There could be no mistaking the bulk of the man, and in the fire glow his hair gleamed like flame itself. Even as the little company watched, Epinard came to the end of his weapons and stood upright, shaking his fist in malevolent defiance. A long war lance arched up from the compound in graceful flight. Rouge Jacques made no attempt to dodge, but wavered only slightly, bracing a foot back, as he was impaled. He stood transfixed a moment longer, silhouetted by the fire, then staggered across the roof and plunged through the rafters where fire had eaten through the shingles. A geyser of sparks shot up.

Fargo turned away; it was a fitting death for a fighter—friend or enemy.

"Let's be rid of here," Celeste urged, squeamish as she continued to wrap Bone's hand with strips torn from his shirt. "If we hurry, maybe we can overtake Father."

"I took him all I can," McHugh grumbled, pressing moss on his flesh wound to stanch the blood. "An' your pa'd take after us, colleen, all he can."

"No, I'm sure he'll listen to reason now, instead of Ives." Plaintively she eyed Fargo. "Your escape so riled him, he was easily persuaded by Ives to go warn Epinard and offer cooperation. Teague was here, a fortnight early, he said, to check some alarming reports about Epinard. He and Father quarreled until Epinard arrived today, looking dreadful, and took Teague captive. It convinced Father he was right, but I believe this'll shake him into thinking again."

Fargo nodded. Not that he agreed wholly with Celeste. Even if Hamilton did change his mind now, he'd likely change back once he reached his fur post—assuming the other free trappers had visited there as planned. Anyway, with Vaurien joined with Chief Quinnalt, it was a reasonable bet that the renegades destroying Fort Providence would strike next at Zashcíta, nearer than Hamilton's Fort George. It was imperative, then, that Zashcíta be warned and manned. There wouldn't be time to search for Hamilton, and besides, it'd serve that conniving Leon Ives right to fight for safety through wilderness with an insane boss for a partner.

Hedging, Fargo replied, "Celeste, I feel we'll meet your dad real soon, but first we've got to get back and patched up." He paused, glancing at the doomed fort. No pursuit bulged from its gate, but as soon as the struggle had died within, the renegades would be out tracking survivors and fugitives. It made their wounds more worrisome, particularly Brusilov's, but there was some consolation in the fact they had a relatively short trek over to their ditched *bateaux* on Libby Creek. 'We've got to keep ahead of those renegade coyotes," he added quietly, standing up. "We'd better get going and keep moving . . ."

11

They reached Zashcíta after a journey dogged by bad luck.

They missed their boats and had to cut back for them. Shooting a twisty riprap, Celeste became alarmed and shifted in her seat, rolling the *bateau* that Fargo was steering so carefully into the current. A day later on the Columbia, a beaver dam broke apart on some tributary above them. The dam must have been of huge size, for the river ran a dangerous crest, tumbling with logs and stumps and debris. They were forced to haul out until the swamping crush was past and the water clear.

Behind them pressed Quinnalt's and Vaurien's renegades. Twice from camps on high ground they could see the fires of their pursuers. Added to this was the fact that even Brusilov had ceased to laugh over his wounds, which were stiffening him now, growing more angry and inflamed. More and more often Brusilov spoke of Netty and Zashcíta. And during the final stretch he often lay delirious, calling out the girl's name with heartrending insistence.

Fargo knew that they should lay up and give Brusilov a day or so of rest. But they couldn't. Nor was there any point even in landing only himself and Brusilov, and letting the others go on. It would be no help to the wounded trapper to save him the rigors of travel, only to let him fall into the clutches of the killers behind.

With deep relief the battered, weary crew beached their craft near the entrance to Zashcíta. Natasha was waiting for them, apparently having watched their approach from the lookout. She darted forward eagerly, but upon seeing Fargo help Celeste from the *bateau*, she stiffened, face clouding, and stalked on up to him.

"Who," she demanded pointedly, "is this old squaw?"

"Who," Celeste asked acidly, eyeing Natasha, "is this brat?"

Fargo made an awkward introduction, suddenly feeling he'd be safer back in Fort Providence. Hastily he said, "Come on, let's get to helping the injured. Brusilov's been hurt pretty bad, Netty, and he'll be needing your care."

Natasha's face paled. She ran swiftly down to where Doyle and McHugh were lifting Brusilov ashore. In a moment she returned. "We'll have to make a stretcher to carry him. And I'll want the cabin clear. Renfrew and Lanarck are in it now. I think you'd better go see them, Skye, and when you do, tell them they can't use it any longer, will you?" Abruptly, without waiting for an answer, she turned away.

Seeing that Doyle and the two women could handle Brusilov and that the rest of the crew would bring in the gear, Fargo went on alone through the tunnel. Entering the pocket, he located Renfrew and Lanarck on the cabin's front stoop. Grim, haggard, in soiled buckskins and legging boots, they glanced up from sorting through a box of scrap musket parts and greeted him dolefully as he approached.

Concerned, Fargo asked, "What's gone on? Where the hell is everybody?"

"They're comin' or sinkin', dunno which," Lanarck replied, shrugging.

"We all went and hit Fort George," Renfrew explained moodily. "Bust in a side door, cut loose firing, and emptied the fur rooms bare. No sign of boss Hamilton, but his men were sure there, more'n usual. They blew the crap outta us before we got away. Runnin' half-crippled with three thousand pounds of fur slowed us, and they weren't long in fixing the boats we holed, then racin' to catch up. We kept 'em at bay, but scraped low of powder, shot, an' suchlike. So me'n Lanarck unloaded our canoes and sped ahead for here, to rig things up and scrounge t'gether any leftover supplies. Don't know how much we gained on our fleet. But short of a run-in on the river, they'll be here anytime now, with the Fort George hounds snappin' at their ass."

It was a bleak outlook, as Fargo contemplated the double jeopardy facing them. "They've shot up Brusilov, and Netty's having him carried to the cabin. Give me a hand clearing out your stuff inside. Then we'll call a palaver."

But in the end, Fargo didn't hold his meeting. There was no question of what should be done and nothing to discuss. The tragedy that Modoc Doyle had asked him to avert was about to occur, needing only the boats to land for a pitched battle between free trappers and fur-company men. Fargo knew the long-run odds favored Hamilton, who could raise more and stronger forces and over time pick off the scattered, solitary trappers. This once, however, the company men were as good as leaderless, not having had any bosses at the fort to go along in charge. So fighting would be unplanned, unordered, impulsive. That'd help the trappers. Mainly, Fargo sensed, that'd ensure that a greater calamity was ready to happen. If they were caught brawling wild by Quinnalt, they'd be ripped down to nothing in nothing flat—except Tahtzi and perhaps Celeste. It'd be a massacre, and the renegades already had Fort Providence as coup, plenty of firepower, and nothing to hold them in check. They'd wipe out every white in the territory and perhaps even spark a general uprising of Northwest tribes.

When Brusilov was bunked down in the cabin to Natasha's satisfaction, and Fargo was sure nothing more could be done for the old trapper right then, he went over to Doyle. "Let's get the men together. Won't hurt to check over things, and see the horns are full and there's shot in the bags. I wish Bone wasn't so mum about his finger. If he's hurting badly, maybe he ought to stay to help Netty with Brusilov."

"Just give Abel his druthers," Doyle advised, and shook his head wearily. "Are we really goin' out to take on them Klickitat?"

"We're going out to meet them," Fargo stated flatly. "We're going to give them hell. Almost everybody is on the way back, shot to the devil but loaded down with Hamilton's plew. The Fort George crew is right behind. We've got to keep the entrance open and make sure those company men don't team up with Quinnalt."

Doyle shrugged with a sardonic smirk. "Ever hear a gent boast he don't get enough of fightin', I'll sure as hell know who to send him to after this."

Minutes later, armed and grim-faced, half a dozen men filed out of Zashcíta, leaving behind them a wounded man and two women. When they reached the river, they split into two groups: Lanarck, Bone, and McHugh were to work along the far side of the river; Renfrew, Doyle, and Fargo were to take the near bank. Before they parted, Doyle reviewed the situation.

"We're guessing there'll be perhaps fifty Klickitats

and a dozen of Vaurien's Canucks. They'll be in canoes, searching for our hide-hole. We ain't about to turn 'em away, but we can confuse 'em and lure 'em upriver for a spell. Soon as our crew from Fort George shows up, Netty'll send 'em out here. We'll have enough guns to do some good with, then. But we've got to draw off this attack till they get here. The first six canoes that pass, you boys on the far side take. Empty them as clean as you can. The next six we'll take, and so on, staggered that way. If and when they land, give ground and dig in upriver, so they'll come after us, thinking we're fallin' back instead of headin' away from the tunnel. It's worth a try anyway."

They moved off then. Every man knew what he was facing and how the odds stacked, but to go by the manner and expression of the trappers, there was wilder danger in a tussle between girls in pinafores. When the trio across from Fargo reached the far bank, he started forward with Doyle and Renfrew. In twenty minutes a whistle sounded on the far bank, and in a moment a fleet of canoes darkened the silver sheen of the river. Squatting in the brush, nerves taut as bowstrings, they waited.

Canoes began to pass. When the sixth one had cleared, flame stabbed from the far bank, causing sudden havoc among the paddlers in the first craft. The long guns spoke again and the second canoe overturned. Then the second section of six drew abreast, and Fargo's fingers curled about his own trigger.

For five minutes they poured a two-sided fire into the confusion among the canoes. Filtering through the rout of cries and rifle shots could be heard the forceful commands of one very tall, very wrinkled old Klickitat—Chief Quinnalt himself, Fargo felt sure, untangling his men and swinging many of the canoes ashore. Answering fire grew stronger. Five canoes landed a few rods below where Fargo and his companions crouched. It was time to move.

As they rose, turning, Renfrew gave a startled grunt and pointed downstream. Two braves were back-paddling their canoe in close to the bank, but unlike other retreating Indians, they had a white man propped in the bow.

"Ulysses Teague," Doyle whispered. "Why've they kept him alive?"

"He's important, valuable as a hostage or to torture when they have time," Fargo said, sliding toward the water. "He's worth taking, okay. Cover me."

"You crazy jughead, you can't!"

Fargo ignored the rest of Doyle's blistering rebuke as he snaked down to the water. Teague was a big man with big holdings in these parts, and saving him could make the difference in saving the free-trapper trade.

Plunging into the river waist-deep, Fargo waded swiftly out toward the canoe. The two renegade paddlers, all that remained of a large crew, turned desperately. One raised a rifle and triggered point-blank at Fargo, but the brave had neglected to charge it with a ball when he loaded. The shot was a plume of smoke. No lead traveled with it. By then Fargo had the gunwale of the canoe, and lunging, grabbed the rifle barrel and yanked the brave into the water. Splashing ungainly, the brave abruptly loosed his hold on the rifle and pawed for the hatchet in his waisthand. Fargo didn't counter or try to protect himself against that menace, but swept in with a straight thrust of his knee. As the brave swerved, the blade slid hilt-deep into his neck.

Withdrawing his knife, Fargo surfaced by the gunwale again and began hoisting himself aboard. Suddenly he ducked, gunshots from Doyle and Renfrew lancing close and low overhead. The second brave glimpsed him then, just at the moment he was busy blasting at the shore; the next moment slugs ripped through him, and spurting flesh and blood, he toppled overboard.

The firing drew fresh attention. When the Klickitats saw that their prisoner was escaping them, they brought their assortment of weapons to bear, indifferent now to whether Teague was killed or not, so long as his rescuer was hit. Their bullets ricocheted and whined around Fargo as he drove into the bank, and a broad swath of arrows rained down, stabbing all about while he was beaching the canoe. Only the Indians' lack of experience with firearms and the low, overhanging brush obscuring their targets prevented them from riddling Fargo and Teague.

Tied hand and foot with rawhide thongs, Teague needed Fargo to lift him from the canoe. Doyle and Renfrew arrived when Fargo was cutting the bonds, but Teague refused their assistance as he struggled unsteadily to his feet. A tiny man who, when standing, barely came to Fargo's shoulder, he wore the tatters of a dark wool traveling suit. It contrasted sharply with pale, almost translucent skin that was pulled taut and thin over delicate bones. His size was misleading, Fargo sensed; Teague was hardened, sharpened steel.

With Doyle breaking the way, they dropped hurriedly back from the river and worked upstream. Behind them, the firing died off. A quarter of a mile above where they'd first struck, an owl hooted on the far bank.

Doyle sent a passable imitation back in answer. "McHugh," he remarked, "just lettin' us know we're opposite 'em and set for another brace against Quinnalt."

"No sign of the others?"

"Skye, if they was in a couple miles and heard that owl, they'da done what I did. You'da thought this was owl heaven for all the birds in it." Doyle spat and dropped a ball into his rifle ahead of his ramrod. "Nope, they just ain't showed yet. That's all."

Moments later the undergrowth rustled behind them. Fargo spun, leveling his revolver at a shadowy blur leaping across a little open. A man threw up his hands and landed heavily. Fargo's shot drew vicious return fire, centering on the flash of his gun and winging lead into the brush where they crouched.

Renfrew swore sharply. "Damn splinter off a saplin' in my cheek," he hissed. "Hurt, that's all."

Glancing from Renfrew, Fargo saw Doyle fingering a wet place on the sleeve of his jacket. The brush crackled again and Doyle fired, sending another man down. Across the river a stray shot snapped out and a Klickitat screamed his peculiar, high death cry.

They were making their lead count. But there weren't enough of them and there wasn't enough lead.

Fargo shifted position, moving up with Doyle and Renfrew, who hovered over Teague just in case. He waited a little longer, hoping to hear a rallying cry from up the river, but it never came. Shrugging, finally, he murmured to Doyle, "This's like trying to stop a spring thaw, Modoc."

"I know. We're dying. Slowly, but we're dyin'."

"We'd better slide, then, before we're dead and there's nothing between them and those two girls."

Doyle sighed, nodding. "I'll let the boys across know." He crept down to the water, and a moment later, the loud slap of a beaver's tail sounded.

Fargo had used that signal himself. Loosely, it meant danger, but the trappers across the river would catch on, all right. The woods were alive with Indians. He grew impatient for Doyle's return, and after a time—too long a time—he cautiously followed after. A couple of yards from the riverbank, he spotted Doyle working toward him. Behind Doyle, an overturned canoe lay on the wet shingle, and over its upper edge, two pairs of legginged legs were dangling.

Doyle, approaching, displayed a curve-bladed skinner's knife. "Last time you saw this, it was against my belly." With a mirthless chuckle, he joined Fargo in heading back. "It's Vaurien's. Him and one of his Canucks had that canoe in the bush right beside me when I signaled. They jumped me quick, but I'm a tad nervous t'night. It's possible neither one knowed just where the knife that got 'em come from."

Fargo's lips quirked grimly. Doyle had a thorough way of settling a score. It was good that it was Vaurien who got repaid, too, for if true to breed, his outlaw *voyageurs* would scatter the instant they learned of his death. Even if they did stick by Quinnalt, their style had been crimped now, and the count made a little less top-heavy. For six men, Fargo thought, they'd done a hell of a lot of damage.

"Okay, break for the tunnel," he whispered upon return. "Fast!"

For a while afterward it looked as if the renegades had them circled. Across the river, the three on the far bank had to shoot themselves out of a corner, plunging into the water in a churning, reckless crossing. But they made it, and in moments the seven of them were running downriver toward the clump of brush that hid Zashcíta's gate. Not far behind them but still on the river, the misdirected renegades were regrouping from confused disarray, and soon would be in deadly pursuit.

As they neared the tunnel, Fargo rushed ahead to jerk aside the brush over the opening—and rammed full into the muzzles of a pair of rifles in the hands of two strangers clad like mountain men. It was a toss-up who was the more surprised. The difference was, Fargo had the initiative, his momentum ramming him hard against their rifles. With swift, downstriking hands, he knocked one barrel to each side of him, plowing on between the startled men. At the same instant, the man on his left triggered, and he felt the sear of its charge along his ribs.

"Shit!" Fargo growled, more angered than hurt, having hoped to avoid gunshots that would tip off the renegades. The graze pulled at his left arm as he laced out with his fist, tagging the point of a jaw and dropping his man. Doyle came in from the side, his burly arms wrapping the other man tight. Renfrew jerked the man's belt gun and laid him beside the first with a quick, sure pass of the short barrel.

Teague scowled worriedly. "How bad are you clipped?"

"Flesh wound," Fargo replied, wincing. "Who are they? Anglican?"

"Sure ain't ours or any I seen with Vaurien," Doyle responded.

As he spoke, sporadic gunfire echoed through the tunnel from the pocket of Zashcíta. It made plain what was afoot. Exhausted and hard-pressed, the other trappers had reached the hideout with their stolen furs in hand and their Fort George pursuers at their heels. The fur-company bunch was more organized than he'd guessed, Fargo surmised; somebody must have ordered these two here left behind as sentries. Fortunately they'd obeyed grudgingly, alert only for the sounds of the battle they were missing. Still, it did not bode well, adding to Fargo's unease as he drew the others close in the end of the tunnel.

"Make all the hell you can when we hit the bowl ahead," he advised. "Shout like seventy instead of seven, burn plenty of powder, but throw your shots wide. Don't tag any of the Anglican men unless they turn on us. We'll need them. We've got them from behind now, and probably our guys are across the bowl behind the cabin. Maybe we can make them think they're caught in a trap."

Weary yet resolute, they disarmed the unconscious sentries and hid them in thick brush away from Indians, then plunged on through the tunnel at a striding lope. Short-legged Teague trotted along, toting a sentry's buffalo gun, and when they finally burst roaring out into the pocket, the sedate fur tycoon was brandishing his rifle and caterwauling like a drunken banshee. As hoped, they burst in behind the Anglican line, which was warily advancing while trading fire with riflemen across the bowl. Their raucous uproar, blasting suddenly, unexpectedly, from the echo chamber of the tunnel, struck the cautiously attacking fur men like a tangible shock wave. Some of them wheeled and dropped defensively. The majority froze where they stood, caught short and waiting for a command. At their head, two startled men swiveled around.

Seeing them started Fargo. Almost at the same surprised instant, Doyle, McHugh, and Teague blurted out one of their names, "Williard Hamilton!"

The other was Leon Ives. Fargo's mind stabbed this development into the swiftly forming pattern of events. Hamilton and Ives, escaping Fort Providence by boat, must have fled homeward up the Columbia and run into their fleet coming down. It made matters awkward to have Hamilton back in command. If he were insane enough, being enthused in the mad scheme for a Northwest empire was apt to make him obsessed, ordering his men to fight for conquest. On the other hand, if he were sane enough, being implicated with Epinard in the scheme was apt to make him desperate, ordering his men to fight against all odds.

"Teague!" Hamilton shouted, stepping forward

with bristling rifles covering him. "I see it now! I see *you* now, the ringleader of these free-trapper freebooters. You sent your scum into Anglican preserves, looted my trap lines, killed my men from ambush, and threw the whole fur country into confusion. I bore your meanness. I was long-suffering. But when you sicced them against my post in open warfare, you broke the covenant, by God! I'll give you five minutes to surrender your entire camp in here to me."

"Hamilton!" Teague stood straight and proud, fair target for Anglican guns. "The lie you've just spoken is no more despicable than your conduct this past year. Anglican came into Yankee territory, murdered our trappers, and stole their catch. You cahooted with Rouge Jacques, you and your subfactor, aiding his mutiny against me. I would die a hundred deaths before I'd surrender the sweat off my brow to you."

Some of that Hamilton could not refute. Frowning, he seemed stymied for words, and his eyes, Fargo decided, were changing, less feverish, less maniac. In the second's hush, footsteps made Fargo glance at the cabin. Both girls were hurrying anxiously from the stoop, Natasha heading toward the trappers, Celeste aiming for the knot of men about her father. Unaware, Hamilton stood glaring and thoughtful, his men hanging upon his withheld word. Fargo took the silent pause as his chance and moved out into the open between Hamilton and Teague, catching their attention.

"You're both wrong," he snapped, hating this sort of orating, really hating it, but having no choice. "And the rift between you is precisely what Red Jack Epinard worked for. Even in death, he is laughing at you. Anglican, Yankee, free trapper, you all suffered murdered men and looted caches, and they all were his work. And the sign he left was

144

to hurl you at each other's throat. Well, go ahead. But you'd be a lot smarter to throw in together, because real soon we're going to be ass-deep in Indians."

"Wha-at?" Hamilton's surprise was echoed by his men.

"Quinnalt's renegades. In five minutes, five seconds, soon."

A yammer of excited comment ripped through the Anglican men, and that got the trappers mingling, explaining. Amazing, Fargo thought, how fast a common enemy can bury hatchets. It was too much for Hamilton; he couldn't bring himself to admit defeat, although he already looked beaten, battered, deserted.

Celeste came and took her father's arm, guiding him gently toward the cabin. Fargo, who happened to be standing close by, heard the man mutter, "They were too many. Take me home, pet, take me home."

"That left Ives standing there flat. When Fargo chanced to glance at him, Ives snarled, his lips curling back from pearly teeth, his eyes shining with the heat of vindictive hate. Patently he blamed Fargo for everything going wrong: Fargo turned away, feeling a certain satisfaction. He located Renfrew and Lanarck, and sent them among the Anglican men with orders to get them up on the slopes on either side of the tunnel. McHugh he sent to round up the free trappers and brace them at the upper end of the pocket. He ran across Natasha then and asked about Brusilov.

Natasha shook her head. "But he hangs on. He wants to see you and Doyle and a few others, after the guns are quiet."

"Well, tell him to hang on. It'll be over shortly."

Natasha turned back to the cabin. Fargo saw Ulysses Teague start in the same direction, but then, apparently seeing the look on the girl's face and the concern in her eyes, Teague fell back. A little later, he saw Teague and Doyle take corners of the cabin, ready to turn the Indians away from the two women and the wounded men who were within it.

All these things took brief moments that ran together into quick flash of time. Then a roar came out of the tunnel, and after it, the red, relentless tide of Quinnalt's warriors. They poured into the pocket, widened, and bounded forward, throwing up their rifles. As the last of them loped out of the tunnel, a party of the Anglican men dropped down, closing off their escape.

Quinnalt hesitated, indecisive. Then he leaped on ahead, followed by his younger braves, who loosened a terrible volley of lead as they headed toward the cabin. It was like the wily old chief to realize that in this shelter were the things his enemy wanted most to protect.

Trappers and company men opened up with barrages of vicious crossfire from both sides. The unexpected fusillades confused the renegades, and they panicked, seven of them dropping in that initial moment before they could react. By then the free trappers were up to their old fighting habit of wading in for a brawl. They charged with pistols and rifles blasting away, yelling encouragement to one another as they mowed into the renegades. More Indians fell as they instinctively dived for cover—of which there was little on the pocket floor—while others stood their ground, firing back at the marauding trappers.

Fargo, sprinting through an arrow-kicked hail of rock shards and grit, answered with a salvo that hit a renegade in the chest. The man sank earthward while Fargo, pivoting, glimpsed Abel Bone, his face contorted, eyes maniacal, his injured hand more capable than most as he capped and shot his single-shot cannon of a rifle. Not far beyond was Renfrew, self-reliant and oblivious to his own safety as he downed one Indian, then swiveled and shot two more who were circling to strike his blind side. Another three renegades were trying for the cabin again, until Doyle stopped them dead with well-tossed lead.

As Fargo continued to turn, he glimpsed peripherally a revolver pointing toward him, the weapon suddenly blossoming flame. He felt the hard slam of the slug as it touched his shoulder in passing, and pulled the trigger of his Colt. Leon Ives reeled from behind a sapling, ran a half a dozen paces more, dropped his revolver, stumbled, and rolled almost to Fargo's feet.

The initial flurry had helped to even the odds, but now there was no more catching the renegades by surprise. Trappers and company men plowed in, slaughtering with merciless desperation. And paid for it, especially in the intense action around the cabin. Lanarck's left ear was torn off by a bullet; howling, incensed, he sprayed the offending renegade with quick one-handed gunnery with his double-action Starr .44, clapping his free hand to his temple to stanch the spew of blood. McHugh was hit simultaneously in the right biceps and thigh, and toppled with his rifle blasting straight up in the air.

Then a fluke. A ricocheting bullet, almost spent, burrowed into Chief Quinnalt's side, lodging in his lower abdomen. A sudden hacking cough, a slackening of his body were immediate signs of the wound, but Quinnalt refused to give in, crawling despite the agony, cutting down two Anglican men with a pistol someone had chanced to drop, before sprawling against a boulder, both hands pressing against his belly.

Fargo couldn't tell which of the free trappers had been wounded. The fight was shrouded by darkness, a swirling fog of night and earth, lit only by the staccato stabs of fire erupting from muzzles of guns. He triggered his revolver until it clicked empty, then used his knife to fend off renegades until he could reload. His was a simple problem: live from one instant to the next. Add up the instants and he'd live to fight again.

The renegades, disorganized and stunned by the loss of their chief, wheeled like a drilled company and raced toward the tunnel. But the Anglican boys were ready. A wall of fire smashed into the renegades, turning them. They made another wild dash, trying to cut through the pall of powder smoke hanging like a curtain before the tunnel mouth. Then a secondary chief threw down his rifle. The Klickitat followed to a man, and firing ceased in the little haven as swiftly as it had begun.

12

Skye Fargo leaned on a discarded rifle like a cane, surveying the miniature battlefield. The Indians were all dead or dying. A half-dozen or so of the trappers and company men were still upright, plus himself. The others were slumped around tending wounds of one degree or another.

Wearily Fargo turned toward the door of the cabin, recalling that Brusilov had wanted to see him when the guns were silent. Natasha opened the door. When he stepped inside, she caught up his hand and led him across to where Brusilov lay on a bunk. One look at the old Russe's face was enough. There was nothing in it now, even the flush of fever having gone. Only his eyes were alive and the shadows of the Divide were gathering in their depths. There was little a man can say to a dying friend, but Fargo felt a deep warmth that Brusilov had considered him to be that good a friend. He lifted Brusilov's hand. A faint pressure ran through the limp fingers.

"The last trail," Brusilov breathed. "Now I go back to the book I t'row away. No matter. I like the she-wolf. With her back broke she stay with her cubs till they are weaned, then she crawl in hole and die. I can do no more for Netty. I t'ink maybe nobody can, heh? Is finish now . . ."

Brusilov caught his breath. For a moment longer his eyes held on Natasha's face, passing on to her with their fading look his devotion. Fargo's arm slid around Natasha's shoulders. The breath eased from Brusilov and he was dead. Fargo turned Natasha, walked slowly with her to the door.

Doyle met them there. "I've got Quinnalt propped up around the corner, Skye. He wants to make palaver, and you might want to listen in on this."

Fargo rounded the cabin with Natasha at his side. The old chief was braced up in state, five or six of his younger aides at his feet. Celeste and Hamilton stood a short distance away, and Ulysses Teague was crouched close to Quinnalt. The chief waved a feeble hand to Natasha, beckoning her close beside him.

"Old men must talk before they can die," Quinnalt said slowly. "The years weigh down their souls with many things. Hear me. When I was a young warrior, the first whites came among us in search of furs. I saw in my mind's eyes a coming time when there would be many whites and no red man. When that time came, my nation must fight or make a shrewd trade. Therefore, I took a party to the lodge of the greatest of the fur men and stole a girl-child from him. I named her Tahtzi and keep her as hostage for the land the whites would take from my people. Then some seasons past, she was stolen from me by a woods runner who kept her as his daughter. I made many attempts to take Tahtzi back, and failed. Now it is too late for my nation, now it is too late for me. I want to return the girl to the lodge of her father—here!"

The old Indian's hand reached out, stabbing a finger at Ulysses Teague.

Teague came slowly to his feet and took Natasha

by the hand, helping her to stand, puzzled, tremulous. "Daughter," he said hoarsely. Then he was more gentle, carefully holding in check the strong emotion pulling at his face. "I've known you since I first saw you, Rosalie Teague."

Watching the two of them, Fargo could not understand how anybody might have known. Their features, as far as he could tell, had absolutely nothing in common, but whether they did or not, it was an unimportant detail. Natasha went to Teague with uncertain eagerness, needing his comfort to fill the void left by the death of Brusilov. From Teague's arms she sent a blinding, happy smile to Chief Quinnalt.

Then Teague spoke again. "I heard, late last fall, whispers of a scheme of lawless empire in these woods. One of my posts, Fort Providence, was involved, and my factor was apparently the ringleader. Then some Indians got hold of them . . ." He paused to give Quinnalt a mockingly stern look. "Well, I've other posts, but your people have only one hunting ground. I'm going downriver with my daughter, and I'll probably return alone. But I'll not rebuild Fort Providence. The territory once controlled by that post I give you in return for my daughter."

Quinnalt's eyes kindled, but his face was graven. "It is good land. My people are grateful. We are a worthy enemy, but are better friend, and as long as honor lives among us, there will be peace."

Fargo smiled. It was a moment for smiles, but in the back of his mind he had doubts. No history book would record this peace. It was without formality, without foolscap, ink, and quill, relying solely on good will, respect, and honor. This area was already a territory, and in not too many more years would come statehood, and government with it. And lawyers and politicos, guaranteed certain death for honorable agreements.

Doyle came by, grousing tongue-in-cheek. "Damn! Lived half a life on the practice that a dead Klickitat was somethin' to be proud of. I was plumb enjoyin' seein' that ol' devil, Quinnalt, fadin' out like a wet fire. Then Teague give him that land, and mark my words, he'll be on his feet in a week. An' I'll have to get me a new mark to practice my shootin' eye on. There ain't a crooked bone in that ol' renegade's body, and what he says, he'll stick to. Be no sport in meetin' a Klickitat on a trail no more."

Fargo grinned, slapped Doyle's shoulder with the affection of a man who has been through a high-water hell with another. Williard Hamilton and Celeste came up before Fargo left with Doyle. Hamilton stared at his feet mostly and didn't speak, and Celeste tried hard to sound optimistic and confident.

"I really must get Father out of this region. I had in mind a nice sanatorium in a warm climate—say, in New Orleans, where he can rest and unwind from strain. Then I plan to return and run Fort George right, widen it out and open it to free trappers. But, Skye, I could use your help in traveling now. Anglican will pay, don't worry, but I want to leave soon as possible. Can you?"

"Well . . ." Fargo glanced at Doyle, whose seamed face was split into a wide grin.

Doyle said, "You're free. You've worn out your welcome anyway." He laughed. " 'Sides, what do I need you for now? The free trappers will have a post in the Northwest, did you hear what she said?"

Fargo nodded. "You and some of the boys, then, better sort out the take you all brought here. Give Celeste a good start in opening up. And Celeste? You might put Modoc in charge of your post till you get back. He'll have it purring for you when you and your father return."

"We might be delayed a season. If that is no problem . . ."

"No, indeed, ma'am," Doyle shouted. "Give me room. I'm an old mountain man with a belly full of war and a hankerin' to settle down."

Fargo moved away.

Natasha saw him coming and moved out to meet him, and when he told her he'd probably be leaving tomorrow, she teased, "With the grandmother, eh? Maybe when I'm an old crone you will like me. But for now, if you come with me, I'll show you a very nice pelt, my fur pirate."

Together they walked down toward the tunnel that would take them outside. They said nothing more. Presently Natasha began to sing,

> Hunters of the fur—
> Live forev-ver . . .

LOOKING FORWARD!

**The following is the opening section
from the next novel in the exciting
Trailsman series from Signet:**

THE TRAILSMAN #69:
CONFEDERATE CHALLENGE

*1860, far west in Kansas Territory,
where the Rocky Mountains rise from the
Great Plains, and men search for
gold and excitement . . .*

Skye Fargo had ridden hard to arrive in the adjoining camps of Denver and Auraria City. The bad weather that had followed him across five hundred miles of barren plains had settled into a cold, gray drizzle. And the avenues of these two fledgling Kansas Territory supply centers were mired in mud.

Since this new gold rush, there was some talk about turning this region into its own separately governed territory, although Fargo thought the idea a bit premature as his Ovaro struggled in a river of muck. But the sounds of building—pounding, shouting, cursing—greeted Fargo in spite of the dreary conditions. On both sides of the street, tents vied with freshly hewn, newly built, false-fronted buildings to create a chaotic, bustling business district.

With his jet-black fore and hind quarters stiff with drying mud and his brilliant white midsection stained brown, Fargo's handsome but weary Ovaro threaded his way between wagons and horses. Now that there was a definite gold strike up in Idaho Gulch, the future of Denver, or perhaps of Auraria City—the two towns were still fighting to take the lead—seemed assured. Men were pouring into the Front Range mining camps. It was said to be so crowded that men slept in shifts in the few available dwellings.

But Fargo had taken precautions. Waiting for him at the edge of the ramshackle downtown was a warm, dry cabin. It probably wasn't much, Fargo admitted to himself, since there didn't seem to be much to the infant twin cities, but at least he would have a quiet, private place to wash off and sleep away the residue of a long trek.

From beneath the canvas awning of a restaurant tent, a man dashed out across a plank sidewalk, splashed in knee-deep mud, careened in front of a startled wagon team, and came to a halt next to Fargo's Ovaro.

"You Skye Fargo?" the man shouted, looking up into the stranger's lake-blue stare.

"Yeah," Fargo answered.

The man's flushed face broke into a grin as he wiped his hand on the soiled apron he wore over his baggy trousers. "I'm Drew Dawson," the man said, extending a damp palm to shake Fargo's hand. "I can't believe you really got here so quick. But I done just what you asked in the letter. Sent my Sally over not an hour ago to start a fire and get a tubful of water heating. Place should be real cozy by now."

The man's eyes sparkled with excitement as he pumped Fargo's arm with an exuberance that would have toppled a lesser man from his horse. "So you come all the way from the Dakota lands since last week." Dawson shook his head disbelievingly. "See any redskins?"

"Yeah," Fargo admitted.

"I hear them Sioux are pretty unpredictable. And the Cheyenne are right rambunctious nowadays. Did you shoot some?"

"Nope," Fargo denied, his tiredness giving way to an amused smile. "I guess I smelled too bad for them to get too close."

"Oh," the man sighed, reluctantly backing away as he accepted Fargo's hint. "You'll be wanting to settle in now, I suppose. The place is right on this street. Last cabin left." Dawson's eager grin returned. "Sally and me would be right pleased to have you to dinner tonight."

"I ate on the trail," Fargo told him. "Tonight I sleep. But I'm obliged for the invitation." Nudging the Ovaro, Fargo left the man behind.

The waiting cabin was a small, haphazardly built affair, its small stoop rising from a sea of mud, but out of a precariously tilting stovepipe on the roof, a stream of welcoming blue wood smoke rose into the misty day, promising warmth. Before he went inside, Fargo led the Ovaro around back to where a trough and feed awaited. Then, feeling bone-weary and chilled to the core, with the grit of ten days' journey scratching under his damp clothing, Fargo waded back to the cabin door. Carrying his heavy saddle, he glanced around, but there was nowhere to set the saddle without drowning it, so Fargo kicked the door open.

The place was small and spare, furnished with nothing but an old iron bed, a rough table, one straight-back chair, a lantern, a large tub, and a huge fat-bellied stove with a big kettle of water simmering on top. But the cabin wasn't empty. A woman slept on his bed. The saddle thudded loudly when Fargo dropped it, and the woman sprang from the bed in one lithe motion.

"Oh, dear," she murmured, brushing at her skirts to straighten them. "I do beg your pardon, sir." Swinging around, the woman snatched her hat and gloves from the quilted spread.

She was the most incongruous sight Fargo had seen in a long time. The woman didn't sport hoops. But she was so burdened with petticoats that her flounced yellow sprigged-muslin skirts covered nearly a fifth of the floor space available in the tiny cabin. Her hat trailed bright-yellow satin ribbons, and her white doeskin gloves could serve no possible purpose other than decoration.

For the life of him, Fargo couldn't figure out how she could have gotten to the stoop without trailing her skirts in six inches of mud. But she looked as fresh as a daisy, as if she were all ready to sit on the veranda of a Georgian plantation. And her voice was unmistakably southern.

"You Sally?" Fargo asked.

"No," she answered, looking momentarily confused. "I am Miss Amelia Miranda Parmeter." Abruptly she offered Fargo a coquettish, inveigling smile and held out one limp wrist as if she expected him to kiss her hand.

Fargo ignored it. Sinking back on the straight-backed chair, he began to tug off his boots. "If I'm not mistaken, that's my bed you were sleeping in, Miss Parmeter," he murmured.

"Oh, dear," she whispered. "I am sorry, Mr. Fargo. I merely came in because the weather is so horribly inhospitable."

"So you know who I am," he muttered, glancing up in time to see the woman blush.

Her elaborately pinned-up hair was slightly rumpled from her nap, and wisps of yellow curls tumbled down across her reddened cheeks. She pouted momentarily, then recovered, flashing a wholly beguiling smile. She was extremely pretty, and she obviously knew it.

Stripping off his socks, Fargo went back to ignoring her, but amusement danced in his lake-blue eyes.

"Of course I know who you are, sir," Amelia declared indignantly. "I've come to hire you."

"I'm already hired by a Mr. Bentley," he told her. "I'm leaving tomorrow. But if you'd like to stay until then . . ." Leaning back in the chair once again, Fargo flashed a smile every bit as beguiling as hers.

"Oh, do you mean it?" she blurted. "I would be most grateful, Mr. Fargo. I never dreamed that obtaining accommodations could be so vexatious in this desolate place. And this is so very much nicer than the tent I'm in. So dry," she enthused.

Startled, Fargo watched Amelia Parmeter pirouette around, looking at the dank little cabin as if it were a first-rate New Orleans hotel. He had only expected to see her blush again. "I don't intend to give up my bed," he protested.

"No, of course not," she agreed.

Her words woke him up as readily as a bucket of cold water. Grinning, Fargo rubbed his bearded jaw. "I guess I'd best take a bath," he commented.

"A bath?" she repeated, her eyes darting across the small confines of the cabin. "I suppose you'll want me to leave for a while," she said, sounding disappointed.

"You don't have to," Fargo assured her, suddenly feeling as if he had awoken from a long sleep.

Fargo's blood pounded in his veins, eliminating all weariness. He stood up.

Amelia Parmeter was a pretty thing, little and dainty, and Fargo towered above her. She looked as if she were all dressed up to go to a ball, and abruptly Fargo smiled at the thought of layers of petticoats tossed aside one by one. It would kind of be like opening a Christmas present, he decided, and the occasion would be as rare, since not very many women dressed that way out West.

"Perhaps we should discuss my business matters first, sir," Amelia drawled softly.

Fargo dropped back onto the chair, all his weariness returning. "We have no business, Miss Parmeter. I leave for Utah in the morning."

"Oh, no, Mr. Fargo. I talked to Mr. Bentley and told him you wouldn't be available."

"You did what?" Fargo demanded.

"You needn't worry, sir. Mr. Bentley was most understanding. After all, you are the Trailsman, and Mr. Bentley only needed a guide. Mr. Bentley understood entirely why I required your services more than he did. And, of course," she concluded, "I repaid the gentleman's advance and found him a suitable replacement. A Mr. Davis. I believe you know him?"

Fargo gaped at her in astonishment. "Yeah, I know him. Josh Davis is fine. But it just so happens," Fargo said tightly, "I want to go to Utah. Don't you think you should have consulted me before changing my plans?"

"But, Mr. Fargo," she protested. Amelia Parmeter whirled away, her skirts swirling. She stalked to the head of the bed and fingered the iron bedpost distractedly before she turned away again and walked toward the stove, halting before her voluminous skirts came in contact with the hot metal. Finally, she faced him. She was young and restless, and she had the tense edginess of a cornered animal. "Certainly, I didn't mean to insult you, sir. I fully intend to pay you twice what Mr. Bentley would." She swallowed. Glancing right and left, her eyes scanned the dimly lit room until a shiver shook her shoulders as she forced herself to face Fargo again. "I was desperate," she whispered.

Fargo smiled tiredly. "I'm sure you were," he conceded. "Desperate and used to getting your own way. But it didn't give you the right to arrange my affairs."

"But, Mr. Fargo, I really must find my fiancé."

Fargo's expression hardened. "Goddamn it, Miss Parmeter. I don't chase after errant husbands or fleeing fiancés. Since you seem to know enough about me to change all my plans, you should know that."

"Why, Mr. Fargo," she squealed, "you do me an injustice. Stephen certainly wasn't fleeing. He merely came out West to pursue his profession," she claimed, lifting her chin haughtily. "Stephen's a painter. And he did not leave me, sir. He merely took a trip. After all," she fumed, "our wedding isn't even scheduled to take place until after the first of next year." Amelia hesitated, eyeing Fargo accusingly. "And I'm going to find him," she concluded, her eyes suddenly shining with willfulness.

"Why?" Fargo questioned.

"Because I must," she answered.

"And you're not going to tell me why?"

"It's a personal matter," she said brusquely. "Surely, you don't need to know in order to find him, Mr. Fargo."

"I don't need to know anything about your fiancé,"

Fargo agreed, laughing. "Because I'm not looking for him."

"Oh," Amelia spat, spinning away again, her skirts sweeping out to take up almost all of the floor space between the bed and stove. She paced four steps, but there was little room for her theatrics, so she turned back on Fargo furiously. "A pox on you, sir," Amelia shouted. "I shall not divulge personal information."

"And I'm not asking you to." Fargo laughed ribaldly. "I'm only here for the bath and the bed," he told her calmly. "If you want to share either one of them, you're welcome. As for your information, I don't want it." Fargo stood up and slipped out of his coat.

Amelia gawked as Fargo tossed his coat across the table and began to unbutton his shirt, but she recovered quickly. Fargo could almost hear her mind calculating on the situation, clicking away like one of those little abaci the Chinese shopkeepers in San Francisco used.

"Oh, Mr. Fargo, I am so sorry," she murmured, suddenly consumed by feminine vulnerability. Her hand fluttered at her breast and her wide blue eyes filled with tears. "I most certainly never meant to offend you," she pleaded.

He had no doubt of that. She meant to harness him and get him to do her bidding like some stupid draft animal. Unfortunately, he was too damned tired to outwit her, and too damned intrigued by her heaving bosom to just kick her out. Eyeing Amelia Parmeter sullenly, Fargo tugged his shirt out of the waisthand of his trousers, knowing full well from the look on her face that she was about to attempt to postpone his overdue bath.

"You really shouldn't, Mr. Fargo," she murmured.

"My brother will be here shortly, and I'm afraid he would think your unclad state most improper."

"Your brother?" Fargo burst out, momentarily disconcerted. "Why in hell do I care what your brother thinks?"

The beguiling Miss Parmeter stared at Fargo, looking genuinely puzzled. "But, sir," she drawled softly, "I am aware that westerners are much more lax in their manners than are southern gentlemen, but certainly you have some idea of the proprieties."

Fargo shook his head as he erupted into laughter. He had little experience with southern belles, and he was beginning to thank his lucky stars for that.

"Listen," Amelia commanded. "Why, it's Jeffrey," she said, bustling to the door.

Amelia tugged the door open and leaned out, sending a shock wave of cold outdoor air across Fargo's bare chest. He shivered with irritation, clenching his fists to keep from throttling the woman.

"Jeffrey, Plato," she called. Within two minutes two men tromped into the room.

Younger than his sister, Jeffrey Parmeter shared her facial features, and if anything, he was even more preposterously dressed. His tight blue breeches were topped by a ruffled linen shirt and a navy velvet waistcoat with satin trim. But his high, polished boots were at least laden with mud, and he obviously hadn't shaved in days, although admittedly, the boy sported more peach bloom than peach fuzz. The black man accompanying him was enormous, grizzled, and white-haired, but impressively muscular.

"Oh, you'll be so pleased," Amelia effused at Jeffrey. "Mr. Fargo has most graciously offered us his hospitality."

Amelia flashed Fargo a brilliant smile, and he felt

his ire rise. He'd been taken, he realized. Fargo was crackling with anger, but too dangerously riled to say a word. He felt as though, if he took any action, he would wipe them all out like a band of renegade Sioux. But Fargo didn't need to do a thing. Amelia took care of everything.

"Plato," she ordered, "you bring in the trunks. Oh, and Mr. Fargo desires a bath. Jeffrey, you can help me hang a curtain."

Without pause she went to the bed and snatched a folded wool blanket from the end of the quilted spread. "Oh, dear," she muttered, scanning the room until she spied several nails pounded into the log wall. Whatever pictures or calendars the nails had supported were long gone, and Amelia's eyes lit.

While Fargo watched, the black man carried in two oversized trunks, several reticules, and numerous boxes. Amelia and her brother filled his bath, hung a curtain in front of it, helped the black man situate the trunks, moved the table, spread three bed rolls on the floor, and generally brought total disorder to the crowded cabin.

"Plato, you can serve as Mr. Fargo's valet," Amelia said, seizing control of the men as easily as any cavalry officer. "Use Mr. Jeffrey's things," she ordered.

Fargo stared as the black man immediately started taking toilet articles out of one of the trunks, a towel, soap, a brush.

"And you, Jeffrey, you go back and fetch Aphrodite. I know it's a tight fit, but she'll be so pleased not to have to sleep in that dreadful tent," Amelia bantered. "But of course, Plato will have to sleep in the wagon. He doesn't seem to mind, though, do you, Plato?"

"No, Miss Amy. I don't mind."

Almost in a trance, Fargo let the big black man direct him to the bathtub. He'd been had, he thought as he heard the door slam behind Jeffrey Parmeter's retreat. All he wanted was a hot bath and a warm bed. He'd been on the road for ten days, stopping only to rest the horse, not daring to sleep much himself, traveling alone in Indian country.

Without thought, Fargo stripped down and sank into the hot tub, wearily leaning back to ease his aching muscles. But then two huge hands were upon him, and he sat up, rigid. "What in hell are you doing?" he demanded, swinging around to face Plato.

"Only soaping your back, sir," the black man answered, looking affronted.

"Goddamnit, call your slave off," Fargo shouted.

"But, Mr. Fargo," Amelia said from beyond the curtain, "Plato is merely trying to help."

"I don't need help taking a bath," Fargo growled, rising out of the water like a wrathful Poseidon. "Get him out of here."

"Plato, perhaps you should best leave," Amelia mewed.

The black man came out from behind the curtain and fairly ran out the door, with Fargo coming right after him. Slamming the door on Plato's fleeing form, Fargo turned on the woman, bearing down on her until her back was pressed against the log wall. Her full skirts billowed out in front of her, however, stopping Fargo's advance several feet in front of Amelia's quivering body.

Fargo was huge, naked, and tense with anger. The flickering lamplight played across his wet flesh, illuminating bulging sinew and muscle. Amelia's round eyes widened.

Abruptly, Fargo regained his composure and realized his postion. "You've got a way of managing things, haven't you, Miss Parmeter?" he snarled. "But I'm not so easily managed," he warned her, stepping close enough to displace the full skirts. He towered above her, glaring down at her, giving her just enough room to slide out sideways.

Fargo hoped to send Amelia Parmeter fearfully scurrying out into the mud. But she merely stared. Her dark-blue eyes were level with his chest, taking in the crisp black hair and hardened muscle. Her gaze dropped to his pelvis and her fascination was obvious. Fargo felt himself respond.

Reaching out automatically, Fargo pulled the woman toward him. He felt her stiff petticoats and gathered skirts press into his groin and his arms tightened around her. She was tiny, fragile, easily enfolded in his embrace. He pressed harder and Amelia collapsed against the wall.

Fargo felt the rough logs scraping his forearm as he wrapped one hand in her hair to pull her head back. He kissed her and the urgency of it surprised even him. Lifting his head, he glowered down at Amelia. The look in her eyes was startled and bewildered, but she offered no resistance. Yet, with immense effort, Fargo thrust himself away and grabbed up the towel on the bed.

"You've invited too much company for me to enjoy your attentions," he rasped.

Still Amelia only stared, her eyes round with awe, her lips slightly parted, her bosom rising and falling in unsteady rhythm. She watched as Fargo pulled on his pants, buttoned his shirt, and donned his boots. She didn't say a word when he grabbed his coat and went to the door. Stomping out angrily, Fargo almost collided with Jeffrey Parmeter and a slender black girl.

"Mr. Fargo, where are you going?" the boy asked.

"Out," Fargo snapped. But when the boy's face fell, Fargo added, "To see if I can find a drink in this godforsaken hole."

"Could I go with you?" the boy questioned eagerly.

Fargo eyed Jeffrey Parmeter. The boy was probably seventeen or eighteen—old enough. Stepping aside to let the young black girl walk inside, Fargo saw Amelia still gazing at him through the open door. "Why not?" he answered sardonically as his eyes met Amelia's. "The more the merrier."

The inside of the one-story, false-fronted saloon smelled of fresh raw lumber and damp sawdust. With Jeffrey following intrepidly, Fargo made his way to the crowded bar. The tinny sound of an untuned piano rose above a riotous clamor of stomping feet, hoarse voices, and clinking glasses, providing dubious music as the customers took their turns dancing with the bar girls. There were only three women among the dozens of men, but women were still rare enough in Denver for one to draw an audience.

One of the women slipped away from her admirers and approached Fargo, and he almost laughed out loud at the flushed look of awe on Parmeter's face. Suddenly, Fargo scowled.

"What's the matter, cowboy?" the woman asked.

Fargo turned to her, not liking the label she had chosen to give him, although he knew the woman had only called him cowboy because he wore a western hat and tight denim jeans, unlike the miners who almost invariably chose heavier, baggier trousers, more suitable for their work.

"Everything," he answered succinctly.

"Maybe I could make it better," she offered huskily.

"Maybe. Have you got a bed and a private room?" Fargo asked. He heard Jeffrey choke on his drink, but he ignored it.

"Right this way," she answered, turning.

"How much for the whole night?" Fargo questioned, holding back.

"You must have been on the trail a long time, mister." She laughed.

"I want to sleep in the bed, not screw," Fargo told her, and Jeffrey Parmeter gagged. "God damn it, would you be careful?" Fargo muttered, slapping the boy on the back.

"But, Mr. Fargo," he rasped, "you can't talk that way to a lady. She's, she's . . ." The boy spluttered into incoherence.

The woman giggled hysterically. She was the only remotely pretty one of the three dance-hall girls. Probably not quite thirty, plump but shapely, red-haired, with full breasts bulging from her red satin and black lace costume, she was attractive in a brassy way. But her hair was freshened with henna and the coppery color clashed badly with the red dress. And her skin looked too pale, almost sickly, in contrast to the black lace.

But she wasn't bad, Fargo thought. She was actually kind of pretty, discounting the unflattering outfit. Fargo glanced down at her overflowing bodice and smiled for the first time. "Well, mostly sleep," he conceded, taking her arm and leading her away.

Jeffrey Parmeter stayed behind, enviously gaping.

Fargo was tired. He lay on the woman's bed watching languidly as she shed her clothing. Her body was generous and fleshy, but not overblown. Her belly was rounded, her hips full, her breasts large but piquantly topped by small, rouged nipples. She smiled knowingly as she lay on the bed beside him and began to remove his clothing. As she unfastened Fargo's belt buckle, he stared into her cleavage. It was deep and dark. She looked soft, and that was what he wanted, a warm soft place to lay his head.

Fargo's organ responded when the woman pulled his pants free and touched him, but he was almost too tired to care. He sat up to help her with his pants, sinking back without complaint when she got up to fetch soap and water. Following a custom perhaps as old as her profession, the woman washed his organ. And Fargo watched her face.

A small furrow of concentration touched her brow. The water was warm, her fingers were slippery, her eyes were luminous green, her mouth was ruby red. But her eyes were a bit too knowing, a bit too harsh, and her skin, framed by a brilliant cloud of red hair, was far too pale, as if it had never been exposed to the light of day. She smiled.

"I guess I pass inspection," he mused.

"Sure do," she agreed. "You can go right to the head of the class."

Turning on his side to watch her plump bouncing bottom as she walked over to the dresser, Fargo laughed at the familiar words, but he didn't feel any undue impatience as she put away her bowl and cloth.

"You look all done in, cowboy," she commented. "Well, not quite," she amended, leaning over to glide her fingers down his turgid organ.

The woman moved around behind him and began to rub his back. Her fingers kneaded at his sore shoulder muscles, traveling up to ease the tension in his neck. Fargo slipped onto his stomach, harboring a vision of toppling the woman down and driving himself inside of her, but he was altogether too content to bother.

"I'm afraid I didn't catch your name," he murmured.

"Clara," she answered. "I didn't catch yours neither," she mumbled. "But then again, most of my friends don't have one."

"The name's Fargo," he offered. "Skye Fargo."

"I've heard of you."

"Good or bad?" he asked.

"Mostly good," she admitted. "But it don't matter none. I know a good thing when I see it."

Smiling, Fargo rolled onto his back, and Clara straddled him. Instinctively, he burrowed his organ into her moist heat. Clara's cheeks flushed as Fargo entered her. Her hips rotated and her eyes glinted beneath her half-closed lids. She was getting prettier by the minute, and Fargo completely forgot that all he had wanted that evening was a bed and a bath.

Clara collapsed on top of him, her billowing breasts pressing into his chest, her fleshy thighs straining against his hard muscles, her hips undulating rhythmically, and Fargo's hands reached out automatically to grasp her buttocks and tighten their bond. The bed was soft, the woman even softer, but Clara wasn't the kind of entertainment a man could sleep through. She rose up over Fargo, tossing her head back and gritting her teeth. Clara moaned. "Please," she pleaded, and Fargo obliged instantaneously.

Grasping her shoulders, he toppled her onto the bed. Following closely, he thrust into her again, pausing to let her catch her breath. But Clara was consumed. Although Fargo blanketed her like a sheet, she struggled to get closer.

She twisted sideways, pressing one fleshy thigh

into his pelvis. She twisted again, shoving her belly against his hard muscle, before embracing him with both legs to bring him in deeper. She pressed hard with her legs, surrounding him like a rigid steel band, but her hips writhed and rolled. Snaking like a sidewinder, Clara gyrated beneath him. Then, bringing her feet down to plant them on both sides of Fargo, she threw her head back, braced her shoulders against the mattress, and bent nearly double, lifting them both off the bed.

Amazed, Fargo realized that in spite of all her softness, Clara rode like a wild mustang. It took a good man to master a mount like her, but he knew he was just the man to do it. Laughing, he pulled back and came down hard, his muscles grinding into her soft flesh.

Fargo plunged into her, forcing her back down, but Clara pushed back. His weight was superior, but she fought it. She lurched. She pitched. She threw herself against him.

They were slippery with perspiration and frothing and foaming with movement. There was no taming of Clara. She was a force of nature, and together they were as turbulent and churning as river rapids.

Clara bucked, surged, and heaved, nearly tossing him off, but he held steady. She made noise like a growling animal, and together they set the bed springs to squeaking with the constant whine of a rusty buggy. Trying to throw Fargo off and hold him close at the same time, Clara gasped and snorted like an angry bull. Then she groaned, and the sound built like a mounting wave, cascading from her like the roaring thunder of white water.

Pressing his thumbs into her hips, Fargo dug his fingers into her buttocks, seeking to imprison her, to hold her still as he rammed into her, driving her hard. But still Clara writhed. Determined, Fargo grasped her hips, holding her down as he slammed into her repeatedly.

Immobilized, Clara strained to keep him inside with her muscles. She squeezed tightly and her muscles quivered. Her thighs held Fargo's slim hips like a vise. Her throbbing muscles surrounded him, and her body pulsated, until Fargo released his hold on her hips, gripped Clara's shoulders, pulled back, and catapulted into her one last time.

Her body shivered, tensed, then seized. And her muscles constricted, pulling the life force from him. Clara screamed and Fargo dropped onto her chest, pressing his face to her hair. She smelled of sweat and musk, his and her own. And he was tired again, pleasantly, thoroughly exhausted.

"You okay?" he mumbled.

"Better," she whispered. "Much better than I been in a long time."

Fargo smiled, thinking that if a man kept a woman like Clara feeling better steadily, he wouldn't last too long. Pulling the bedspread up over them, he stretched lazily, reflecting that it wouldn't be a bad way to go—working every bit of flesh and muscle till it just wore away. Drifting off with one arm slung around Clara's soft shoulders, he was just managing to conjure an erotic image of his own demise when the dream shattered.

A crash sounded in the room, Clara screamed, and a spray of glass rained across them. Instantly, Fargo was wide awake. He pulled Clara over on top of him and rolled off the side of the bed. Fargo landed flat on his back. The hard wood jolted him, and Clara's breasts pressed against his face like a smothering pillow.

Fargo pushed Clara away and shrugged out of the

entangling bedspread as he grabbed for the gun he had left on the chair beside the bed. "Keep down," he shouted at Clara as he pulled the Colt from his gun belt. Fargo turned and dived under the bed, grimacing as splinters from the rough flooring bit into his arms and knees. But he was very careful not to let his pelvis drop.

Inching forward, Fargo saw the man who had destroyed his peace. The man was on hands and knees, still crouching after his flying leap through the window. Fargo thrust his head out from under the bed just as the intruder got to his feet. Before the man could react to Fargo's motion, the Trailsman brought his Colt around and up. Gunfire exploded in the room. The intruder's weapon clattered onto the floor, and his corpse followed, slowly, anticlimatically, making a hollow, thumping sound as it hit.

Before he could quite figure out what had happened, Fargo was standing over the man, staring down at a strange face. The crimson stain on the stranger's chest looked too small to have caused so much damage, but the man was definitely dead when Clara crept up beside Fargo. Fargo glanced at her, and she catapulted into his arms. Clasping her with one arm, he reached back with his other to set the Colt on the bedside table.

"A friend of yours?" he asked.

"No," Clara sobbed, shaking her head against Fargo's shoulder. Clutching at him, she drew great heaving breaths, and her breasts moved against his chest. "I never seen him before," she whimpered. "You sure he ain't a friend of yours?"

"Pretty sure," Fargo muttered. "I suppose he might have known me, or of me. But I didn't know him. And I sure wouldn't have counted him a friend."

Fargo brought his fingers up and tilted Clara's chin back. "You okay?" he asked.

"No," she denied. Her pale skin was tearstained and her green eyes were wet and sparkling. All the knowing coarseness had drained from her face, and she was just a woman in need of comfort.

It had all happened too fast, leaving Fargo as edgy and sensitive as a bristling cat. He could feel the skin prickle across his bare back and shoulders. And he wanted to pummel the bastard who had, for no known reason, robbed him of his well-deserved lethargy. After ten days of hard riding and little sleep, Fargo was brimming with roiling, seething anger. He was fairly shaking with the urge to wring an apology out of the stranger, but a civilized man didn't go around mutilating dead bodies—even if the stinking bastard did still owe him an explanation. Unconsciously, Fargo tightened his hold on Clara.

He felt Clara's soft rounded belly press against his groin, while her clutching fingers groped frantically at his shoulders. A shock of cold air rushed through the newly broken window, setting the woman in his arms to shivering. Turning Clara away from the window, Fargo reached out to push the curtain over the shattered glass. He scanned the darkness as he did so, but there was nothing moving in the lot behind that backroom of the frenzied dance hall. The tinny music straining from beyond the hallway was all Fargo could hear.

Knowing Clara was much more shaken than he himself had been in many years, Fargo soothed her bare back and shoulders. "Ready to face the law?" he murmured.

Clara trembled. "Give me a little time," she

pleaded. "Just a little time. Just stay with me for a few minutes."

Fargo agreed readily. While Clara sat on the bed, he moved around it. He pulled on his pants, then leaned over to fetch the heavy bedspread for Clara, but before he could hand it to her, he was lunging across the bed for the Colt. He grabbed it, shoved himself back off the bed, and landed on his feet with the weapon steady in his hand just as the door swung open and Jeffrey Parmeter stepped into the room.

"I thought I heard a shot," the boy exclaimed. "I wasn't sure. It was so noisy in there, but . . ." The boy stopped and gawked, while color spread from his cheeks to the roots of his light-blond hair.

Clara was trying frantically to escape without taking her eyes off the intruder. Scrambling like an awkward crab, she was trying to move backward propelled by her elbows and feet, with her knees up and her thighs spread, revealing flesh still damp from her earlier lovemaking.

Abruptly, Jeffrey Parmeter seemed to be in a trance. He didn't even notice when Fargo walked between him and Clara's open thighs. Clara pulled her knees together, and Jeffrey stared at her breasts.

Tossing Clara the bedspread, Fargo rolled his eyes in amusement. "You seem to have a fan," he muttered to Clara.

But the sound of Fargo's voice made Jeffrey recall his manners. He looked away, drawing up shortly and gasping as his gaze fell on the intruder's body. "Why, you've shot Mr. Caldwell," the boy whispered.

Fargo glanced up sharply, dropping his hands from the gun belt he was fastening. "You know him?" he demanded, striding back around the bed to join Parmeter.

"Uh huh." The boy nodded dazedly.

"Why? Where? How? How do you know him?" Fargo questioned.

Jeffrey looked at Fargo with glazed eyes. "I met him," he answered tonelessly. "At Dexeter Plantation."

"What's that?" Fargo demanded. "What's Dexter Plantation?"

"It's a home," Jeffrey answered. "It's Stephen Dexeter's home. He's engaged to marry my sister." Jeffrey swallowed as he glanced back at Caldwell's body. "As a matter of fact, Stephen came out here with him." Jeffrey's voice was flat and hollow, echoing his shock. "Stephen is a painter," he murmured. "He came out here to do a portfolio on Indians, an update on Catlin's work."

"So why was Caldwell trying to shoot me?"

"Shoot you?" Jeffrey repeated, turning his bewildered gaze on Fargo. "I'm sure I don't know, sir."

"In that case, it seems I've got some more questions to ask, somewhere," Fargo ground out harshly.

Sitting down to pull on his boots, Fargo turned to Clara. "I'm afraid you're going to have to face the law without me. Tell the sheriff I'll see him in the morning. If the sheriff's heard of me, I don't think he'll make too much of a fuss."

"You'll come see me again some time, won't you?" Clara whispered.

Fargo's smile sparkled in his eyes. "It will be a pleasure," he told her.

Before leaving, Fargo paused to speak to Jeffrey Parmeter. "I think you'd better stay and tell the sheriff what you told me. And as for Clara, I don't think she should be alone tonight. You'll stay with her, won't you?"

Clara had scooted up on the bed, covering herself, but her rounded, ample flesh jutted out from both sides of the sheet she clasped between her breasts.

Staring at her with lustful intensity, Jeffrey Parmeter swallowed hard. "It will be an honor, sir."